BIG BURN

BIG BURN

Lesley Choyce

Thistledown Press Ltd.

Canadian Cataloguing in Publication Data

Choyce, Lesley, 1951-
Big burn
ISBN 1-895449-43-X
I. Title.
PS8555.H668B5 1995   C813'.54   C95-920056-8
PR9199.3.C466B5 1995

Book design by A.M. Forrie
Cover art by Rand Walsh
Set in 11 pt. Garamond
by Thistledown Press Ltd.

Printed and bound in Canada by
Webcom Printing
Scarborough, Ontario

Thistledown Press Ltd.
633 Main Street East
Saskatoon, Saskatchewan
S7H 0J8

This book has been published with the assistance of
The Canada Council and the Saskatchewan Arts Board.

Big Burn

Lesley Choyce

Chapter One

This is how it begins. School is over until September, and I have all summer ahead of me. I'm sitting alone here on the hill as the sun goes down. In front of me is fifty-five acres of garbage. I spend a lot of time sitting here at this dump thinking. Thinking is my worst fault. Thinking and worrying.

After dinner I like to ride my mountain bike through the trail in the forest and come here to where I have a hole cut in the fence. I'm sixteen now and I should be doing better things with my life. But I've been coming here since I was a kid. Back then the dump seemed kind of exciting. I used to find all kinds of good stuff that I took home. Old record players and radios and neat stuff.

Back then was six years ago. I was ten years old. I was just a kid. A dump was just a big hole in the ground that you filled up with everybody's junk. If a kid got lucky he found something worth taking home.

I hear a loud gunshot. *Kapow.* A bullet ricochets off an old stove down in the pit. I nearly jump out of my skin. Then I hear a series of five more gun shots. Somebody yells, "Got one! Killed the little sucker!"

I look over towards the incinerator stack. Two men are standing outside with pistols. They're shooting at rats again. It's what they do on the night-shift when things get boring. They shoot at anything that moves out in the dump.

I don't think they can see me, but I lie low on the ground and stare up at the sky. The plume of smoke that rises in the light of the sunset looks almost pink — warm and pretty, not like in the middle of the day when it looks grey-white and harsh. Now it's almost like some living, cotton candy cloud out of a fairy tale.

The wind will keep me safe, I think sometimes. The wind is my ally. This week, I'll dig out my windsurfer, rig the sail, and be down there on the water — ripping along like last year.

Several seagulls are flying near the smoke now, catching the rising warm air no doubt. I hear three consecutive shots again. The stupid idiots down below are shooting at the birds. Two of the gulls are hit and drop from the sky. A third is frightened and flies off over my head.

The men near the base of the giant incinerator stack are laughing. I can't believe it. A door to the building opens and another man walks out. I recognize him as Mr. Gibson, the man in charge here. One of the guys points to the two seagulls he shot down. Gibson takes off his cap and just laughs. They're all laughing, these creeps. Then Gibson opens the door to the building and they all walk back in.

When the door is closed, I scream at the top of my lungs but no one is around to hear.

I run along the rim of the pit until I find a place I can climb down. I've kept my eye trained on the spot where the two gulls fell. In order to get there, I have to race across a field of dark wet ash. This is what's left over after the incinerator has done its work. It has a frightening lifeless quality — even though it's been compacted before dumping, it sticks to my shoes and pants. I fall once and get it all over my arms and some on my face. "The ash is the worst of it," my father says. "After the burn, the ash is a concentrate of a hundred toxic chemicals."

In the middle of the ash I find one bird dead, a bullet hole through its chest. Nearby, though, the other one is flopping around. The bullet tore through one wing which is now hanging, barely attached by skin and muscle. He squawks the cry of a creature in deep pain. I think of the yahoos working the incinerator and wish I had the means of doing some damage to them.

Instead, I try to capture the bird. This is no easy task. He's big and he's very mad. I throw my jacket over him, and try to tuck the broken wing properly in place just to get him still. He strikes out with his razor-sharp beak and tears through the arm of my shirt and digs into my skin. Let me tell you, it hurts. A mean seagull is not a thing to wrestle with lightly. I howl in pain.

But then I get the jacket over his head. He grabs onto it with his beak but I've got his eyes covered. He can't see. I feel him push away at me with his powerful feet but then he settles down. Together we track back across the path of incinerator ash, up the embankment.

With great difficulty, I carry him under my arm as I ride my mountain bike through the darkening forest on my way home.

I know that there is something different about me tonight. The anger is all tied up with this feeling of frustration. Maybe it's something I inherited from my old man. I remember seeing him just like this — angry and frustrated when he lost *his* battle, two or three years ago, against the incinerator. Under my arm, I feel the rage of the squirming gull who doesn't know why some ugly human force would put a bullet in him and take away his freedom, his life in the wind.

I have brought home plenty of wounded creatures before — a raven caught in a washed-up fisherman's net, a pigeon that was half-starved, even a racoon that had been caught in a leg-hold trap. Sometimes my attempts to save things work, sometimes they don't. I've never believed in that dumb theory of putting an injured animal out of its misery. My parents understand.

"The bone is shattered in three places," my father says when I get home. I am holding the frightened bird as he examines it. It takes all my strength. My mother is wiping the blood off my arm and applying disinfectant.

"The wing can't be set, Chris. There's not enough left. You call it, Son," my father says. I feel tears in my eyes. How often do people talk about the "stupid gulls" that hang around the landfill and annoy everybody in the community? Here's just one stupid old gull that someone shot for the heck of it. What would it matter to anyone if he died there in the ash?

"We'll cut the wing off. I want to do it," I say. I know my father is as squeamish about this as I am right now. I feel responsible.

He gets his long-handled pruning sheers that we use for cutting branches off trees. I take them from him. My father hangs onto the gull and lets it grab onto his glove with its beak. He gently but firmly cradles the gull's head with his other hand.

My mother has retreated inside. I stretch out the shattered wing, study the bone. I suck in my breath, gather the will to do this. I centre the blades over the place where the bone is completely shattered through by the bullet. Again I see that there is nothing holding the wing on but skin and muscle. I gently but firmly cut with the shears.

Chapter Two

I had a hard time sleeping that night. My mom heard me tossing about, I guess, because she came into my bedroom. She knew I was pretty angry about the idiots at the landfill site and about the injured seagull.

"How you doing?"

"I don't know. I can't sleep. I just don't understand why people have to be so cruel."

"Welcome to the club. But don't drive yourself crazy trying to figure it out. You did a good thing."

"But it wasn't enough."

"You sound just like your father."

I thought then of the battles my old man had lost, but I didn't say anything about it.

"We should just move. Get out of here," I said. But I didn't mean it. I loved the harbour in front of my house. I loved life here in the boondocks with forests and water and plenty of elbow room.

"Maybe we will yet," she said. "Now get some sleep."

But I lay there thinking about my old man and how he had been whipped trying to stop the dump. Sure, he had people on his side, but not enough of them. People along this shore never had enough clout to be heard. And then when they pushed the incinerator through, there weren't enough fighters left around here to stand up to it. A lot of them had just moved on to some place still clean, still unpolluted.

The incinerator was supposed to cut down on the amount of garbage going into the ground. Instead, more junk kept coming in from farther away. And now there was the ash, which my father said was much worse than any of the garbage going into the pit.

A week had passed. I named the gull Jack, after an uncle of mine who had his leg blown off by a "friendly" land mine in the Gulf War. Despite his loss, Uncle Jack held on to a great sense of humour. My seagull, however, never quite forgave the world for taking away the feel of the wind under his wings. I kept him in a cage and fed him fish scraps from the IGA. He sure was mean to me but I never held that against him. After a few days, he trusted me enough to eat an old fish head in one gulp straight out of my hand. But every so often he still took a chunk out of me. We had a cautious kind of friendship, Jack and me.

Now he watched me with a curious kind of smirk on his face (or so I imagined) as I got out my windsurfing gear for the first time that summer. Summer was starting to happen and I wanted to get out on the water. With the fin off my board, I set it on the grass and put the sail into place. Jack watched as my sail caught the wind and billowed out for the first time that year. I stood for a few seconds, perfectly positioned — until a big gust came up out of the east and yanked hard on the sail, pulling me clean over onto the ground. My old instincts weren't quite up to snuff. Practice needed.

I put on my wetsuit and carried the board down to the harbour, just down at the bottom of our garden. The wind was punchy and a bit chilly, but as soon as I found my feet and made a clean water start, I was gone. I hooked in my harness, leaned back for the perfect position and let the board spit off up the harbour in the deep, cold, salt water. I disturbed a bunch of Canada geese near the shoreline at Blueberry Point, and they scudded the water with their wings as they took to flight. Then I cranked a turn and headed back out to deeper water and stronger winds where whitecaps made me pull in on the sail and pop over them for a bit of air.

If I hadn't seen a second sail further up the shore, up near the dump, I think I would have gone further out towards the mouth of the harbour and rattled my bones flying over the little waves that were pouring through. But there it was, a beautiful, blue and red windsurfer sail off to the north.

Another jibe, this one with a bit too much wind from the wrong direction. I lost it and settled in the drink with cold, cold water awakening parts of me that had been asleep all winter. How embarrassing! It took a few awkward minutes to get my board around in position, my feet in the straps and my cold, shivering body back under control. But once the wind and I had made friends again, I felt it collect me out of the water and pull me to my feet. We began to get speed just as a magnificent loon popped up out of a deep dive in front of me. I cranked hard on the tail to carve an S turn around it with a word of apology.

Now I'd lost the sail I'd seen before. Where was it? And who was this other brave soul willing to surf the cold waters of my harbour? I cruised north along the shore, wishing I didn't have to travel this way, up near the dump site that came to within five hundred metres of the water. The incinerator stack was right in my sights again. How could I miss it? The cold grey-white plume pumped up into the other-wise blue sky. I was in close to shore and passing the abandoned fishing wharf that the government had rebuilt a few years back. Now it was empty; the fish were mostly gone. The wharf was just a long, ugly concrete arm that stuck out from the shoreline. It served no purpose. Just another eyesore.

I began to wonder if the windsurfer I'd seen was a mirage or if someone had wiped out and couldn't get back up. That happened to every-body at least once. One time I had to paddle my board back nearly a mile to get home — just couldn't find a way to get going in a wrong wind.

I was out of the sea wind now and into a minor light breeze. No whitecaps. I studied the shoreline as I passed beyond the wharf. Deep spruce forests and rocks. But as you got closer to the dump, the trees looked less healthy. The dump supposedly had some kind of liner, something to keep the ash from leaking out. My guess — and it didn't take a genius to make this one — was that it didn't work. Something was leaking, slowly but surely, into the ground water.

Then I saw the sail and the board, beached by the little trickly river we called Bedford Brook. I cruised in close to the shoreline and hopped off into the knee-deep water that had a light film of something on it. I slipped on some slimy rocks and fell over with the sail on top of me.

As I lay there in the mud trying to find my way out from under my wet sail, I could smell the stench — some kind of odour like old tires or diesel fuel. I didn't know exactly. But whatever it was, it was in the water coming from the brook.

When I untangled myself from the wet sheet of my sail, there was a girl standing there. I guess I looked pretty foolish. But she wasn't smiling. She looked mad — real mad.

Chapter Three

"Why did you let them do it?" the girl demanded of me, like I had just committed a crime or something.

"Do what?" I asked. Boy, was I confused.

"How could you people let them get away with it?"

"With what?"

"That, stupid," she said, pointing into the forest, towards the landfill.

I was beginning to clue in slowly to what she was talking about, but I was still wondering if this girl was flipped or what. I had a hard time getting my footing on the slippery stones as I stood up and walked towards her.

"Don't you people realize what that dump and that smokestack are doing? They're killing this place."

I flashed back to hearing my old man, years ago, talk just like that. But here I was confronted with this girl my own age, a girl with long, red hair, and not at all bad looking despite the bulky, black wetsuit she was wearing. And she was lecturing *me* about the dump. "Hey, wait a minute," I said. "It's not my fault."

"My father says this used to be one of most beautiful harbours in North America — or it was when he was growing up here."

"It still is," I said, feeling a little defensive.

"Not with that, it isn't," she said pointing inland to the landfill. "When we moved down here, I thought I was getting away from polluted air and dead lakes. And then I find this. Don't people around here care about anything?"

"My father fought this thing, okay?" I said to her, feeling my voice rising. "So did other people. But not everyone. There weren't enough. The garbage had to go somewhere, I guess. Every other town screamed louder than we did. So we lost."

I could tell I made my point. But I guess I said the wrong thing. The girl gave me a cold look and walked over to her windsurfer.

She grabbed the boom and began to walk it out into the harbour.

"Wait a minute," I said. This girl had me totally mixed up. First she insults me. Then I realize that she is good and ticked off about the same thing I am. I think she's kind of cute and I want to know her name, only I've insulted *her*. And now she wants to disappear in the wind.

"Wait, please," I said, but she was already waist deep in the water and letting the wind in the sail pull her up onto her feet. She executed a flawless takeoff and hitched her harness in as she headed for deep water.

I pointed my board back out to the middle of the harbour and made a clumsy stand-up start, bumping the fin on a couple of big rocks in the water. I wasn't about to let her get away.

The wind was coming in walloping gusts once I got away from shore. I could see the bloom of her Mistral sail heading north, and I gave chase. I cranked hard on the tail and tried to get the board to go for full-on speed. I was thinking that maybe this strange girl would at least be impressed by my windsurfing skill and give me a second chance at conversation.

When I caught up to her I think I surprised her. She didn't realize I'd follow. Coming up close and running parallel to her, I asked, "Where do you live? Maybe we should talk." I wasn't really trying to come on to her. I just felt kind of weird about the way we met. There was more to be said. There was unfinished business.

Instead, she surprised me with a radical turn straight into my path. I had to crank hard around to keep from running into her. That gave the wind full control of my sail and I went flying head over heels into the water.

When I surfaced, I saw she was gone, headed into the deeper water and the stronger winds further out. I had a hard time getting a water start, tried to catch up, but it was hopeless. By then she was flying, bouncing off the whitecaps of the little waves and executing moves that I could only do in my dreams.

I rode my bike down to the gas station and saw Bickman and Grieg hanging out there. "I met this girl on a windsurfer. She must be new. You guys know where she lives?"

Barry Grieg kind of snickered and Bickman looked up into the sky with a grin on his face.

Marina
Ryerson

I immediately regretted asking these clowns anything.

"Sounds like you're pretty interested in her," Barry said.

"Just curious."

"My sister talked with her," Bickman said. "She's got some funny name. What was it? Mary Anne? Mary Anna? No . . . I think it was Marina . . . Marina Ryerson. She and her family moved into that old house that's been empty up at the head of the harbour."

"She's from away," Grieg added, like this was some brilliant addition of information to the story.

I guess I found out what I'd been looking for. "Hey thanks, man."

"What's the hurry?" Barry added, slugging back on a can of Pepsi. "Tell us what she looks like in a wetsuit."

But I was out of there. I didn't feel like hanging around.

So her name was Marina Ryerson, and she had just moved here. She lived up near the head of the harbour in an old house. I went through some pretty sore muscles, cruising the harbour every morning on my sailboard, searching for her. I knew that she was a pretty hot windsurfer and that she'd be in the water again. But I kept my distance. You could see that sail from a long way off.

I guess I was a bit of a snoop. But I wanted to meet her real bad. I knew she wasn't like any other girl I'd ever met at school. It seemed like the girls I had gone out with were only interested in rock videos and make-up. This Marina was different. Even her name was different. On my third try, I tracked her all the way up the harbour, past the dump site, and saw her get out of the water at a little old farmhouse near the highway.

Now, I was never very good at strategies with girls, but I knew that I had better work on something quick. Marina was, well, unique. And I had a hunch we were a lot alike. I decided that maybe Jack could help me out.

So, on Saturday, I put Jack in a little wire cage designed to transport cats. I strapped it to the back of my bike and rode down the road, all the way to the head of the harbour and the little farmhouse. What was left of the stub of Jack's wing was healing up amazingly quickly. It was still kind of depressing to think of a seagull with one wing who would never be able to fly again.

I had to keep looking back to make sure he was okay. He wobbled about in the cage a bit as I rode but then he got his balance and I think he liked it — maybe it was as close to flying as he'd ever get again, whizzing down the road on the back of my bike with the wind in his face. He could push his beak through the cage wire, and twice he gave me a mean bite in the butt before I positioned him so he couldn't get at me.

With Jack in his cage under one arm, I knocked on the door. The house seemed very quiet.

She came to the door. She had on an old flannel shirt and dirty jeans. It looked like she had been working on something.

"Hi," I said. "I wanted to introduce you to a friend."

She looked at Jack and then at me. "What did you do to it?" she asked accusingly.

"Cool it, will you? I didn't do anything to it but save its life. He's only got one wing."

"I can see that," she said.

"The guys who work the night-shift at the incinerator. They have guns and they pick off rats and birds — for kicks."

"That's sicko," she said.

"That's what I think. I was there one night and I saved this guy." Jack stuck his beak out through the cage and tried to chomp off my finger as I pointed at him. "I thought you might know something about seagulls."

She shook her head. "Not much. They eat fish. They're supposed to have two wings."

"His name's Jack," I told her.

"Hello, Jack," she said.

"I'm Chris," I told her.

"Marina," she said.

And that was the chance I'd been waiting for, a chance to have a complete conversation with Marina Ryerson before the wind took hold of her and raced her away.

Chapter Four

She didn't invite me in, but she walked over to an old picnic table along the shore of the harbour. I set Jack's cage down on the table and sat down beside him. From here you could look straight down the harbour, all the way to sea. It was a magnificent view — if you could ignore one thing. We both tried to avoid looking at the dark finger of the incinerator stack on the western shore.

"If you could only pretend that it's not there . . . " she said.

"They say it's high enough so that nothing from the burn actually comes back down here. It gets pumped into the prevailing wind and goes off, out to sea." It sounded a bit too much like an apology for the incinerator.

"Everything comes down somewhere. If we don't breathe it, someone else will. Or it will come down in the rain. Into the sea. Kill some fish. Or do something worse."

"You know, the dump has been there ever since I was a kid. I couldn't do anything about it. Heck, I even used to think it was a good place to hang out, to find neat junk."

Marina smiled. "I guess I know it's not your fault," she said. The sunlight was dancing through her long red hair. Marina caught me staring.

"My mother and father fought against it and lost," I told her. "Then when they started talking about expanding the site, everybody jumped up and down in opposition. My father still had his job with the Department of the Environment then. He was in on it. 'Burn the junk,' the hot shots said. Saves land, saves money. It's clean and you can even produce electricity. So the story went. It sounded great, I guess. But my old man didn't think so. He read some research reports. He visited some other incinerator sites. He knew it wasn't that simple."

"But he let them get away with it anyway?"

"No. He went to the media. He knew that these things weren't as clean as they were cracked up to be."

"Good for him."

"Yeah, good for him. Except that nobody listened. And he lost his job. Now we scrape by on the money he makes from free-lance writing. My mom has to work too. He stuck his neck out and had it chopped off."

Marina picked up a rock and threw it in the water. She had that angry look on her face, like when I first met her. Time to change the subject. I wondered why I was sitting around talking about garbage with a girl that was so good-looking.

"You just moved here, didn't you?" I asked.

Marina sucked in her breath. "Yep. My father wanted to come back here where he grew up. He loves this place. We were living in Culverton."

"Great place."

"Ever been there?"

"No."

"I guessed that. Culverton is not a great place. It has a lot of old factories — big ones."

"And that's why your father wanted to move back here," I said. "He remembered this place the way it was when he was a kid."

"Well, something like that. We weren't exactly living at Love Canal. But the whole area around Culverton . . . well, the air and the water were polluted. Nobody cared enough to clean it up."

"Yuck. I can see why you wanted to move."

Marina suddenly looked troubled, defeated. "C'mon, I want you to meet my father. Bring Jack."

I followed her inside through the old farm kitchen, past the wood cookstove.

"I love the feel of this place," I told her. I meant it. It reminded me of my grandmother's house, an old storey and a half saltbox heated by two wood stoves.

In the living room, a pale looking man was sitting in a Lazy Boy recliner watching TV. Alongside him was a table with a bunch of tools and some strange looking little mechanical contraptions. As soon as we walked into the room, he clicked the TV off with his remote. But when he smiled at me I knew that something was wrong. It wasn't just the pale skin of his face. It was something in his eyes. It was pain I was seeing.

"Dad, this is Chris," she said.

"Hello, Mr. Ryerson."

He smiled at me, then looked at the cage.

Marina took Jack's cage and showed him to her father. "Some creep shot his wing off," Marina told him.

Mr. Ryerson took an immediate interest in Jack. "Hold him up closer here," he said.

"Watch out, he'll try to bite," I said, realizing that "bite" wasn't exactly the right word.

Marina's father was studying what was left of the stub of the wing. "It doesn't look infected. Is he eating?"

"Like a horse," I said. Jack could eat three pounds of fish heads at one time.

"Good. Gulls are survivors."

"Yeah," I said. "I just wish that there was some way he could fly again."

"Still, he'll be able to go in the water. Gulls can float and dive. He can be a water bird."

"Right."

"And you never know. He's got a stump there for a wing. You never know."

But I knew. I had lopped off seventy-five percent of the wing. This was not a bird who was going to fly again.

"You need anything, Daddy?" Marina asked.

"Not a thing."

I thought I should try to make a stronger impression. "What's the stuff on the table?" I asked him.

Mr. Ryerson lit up into a smile again. "Inventions," he said. "Little mechanical contraptions that I make up out of my imagination."

I looked at these odd little gizmos that were made up of metal arms, plastic, gears, and wheels — all in the strangest shapes.

"What do they do?" I asked.

"Most of them don't *do* anything at all. But they help keep my mind alive," he said, thumping the front of his skull with his forefinger.

"Oh, I think I get it," I said.

"Good," he replied, clicking on the TV again. "Now you two get out of here. Too nice of a day to be inside. Off with you." But he wasn't being nasty. It was something else.

We went back outside and walked along the edge of the harbour, finding beached mussel shells, cracking them open and feeding the insides to Jack who gobbled them up.

"I like your dad," I told Marina. But what I really wanted to ask was what was wrong with him. I didn't quite know how to approach the subject without maybe making her feel real uncomfortable.

"I'm glad we could move back here," Marina said as she watched Jack. "I just wish he could enjoy the place more."

I didn't know exactly what the right word was to say. "Sorry."

Marina shook her head. "I wish people would stop saying that," she suddenly snapped at me.

I was afraid to say anything else. I waited. The wind was coming up off the sea now. Little wavelets slapped at the stones beneath our feet. Jack seemed to come to full alert from the smell of the salt in the air.

"He worked at a chemical plant for twenty years. He always said it was a good job. Dial Chemical, it was called. Ever hear of it?"

"Never."

"It was a big company. My dad said it was a good place to work. He believed in it. He even saved some money and bought some stock or something. I could never understand how he could feel that way about that awful place."

I nodded my head like I understood, but I wasn't sure what she was talking about.

"We lived only a couple of blocks away. The air always smelled. He always smelled bad when he came home from work. And it seemed like my mother could never wash the smell out of his clothes or get it out of the house.

"Then, last year, he started getting sick. It started in his kidneys, then it was his lungs. Now . . . " Her voice trailed off.

Her father wanted to come home to die, I realized now. And he wanted to get his family away from whatever it was that was killing him.

"We had a lawyer but we didn't get anywhere. He couldn't prove that it was the job. The company lawyers said he could have got sick for any one of a hundred reasons. The system sucks," she said.

She was looking far down the harbour again. The wind rippled through her hair, and I knew that I had landed more than I had bargained for. Part of me just wanted to back away from her, to go home, and not get involved. I just wanted to go racing my mountain bike through the forest or go catch a spit of wind and cruise around on my sailboard. But I couldn't do that.

She turned to me now. I could feel how tense she was, how angry. It was like a kind of electricity coming out of her.

"My father loves this place — this harbour, this coast. If people don't fight, it's going to be like where we came from." She clenched her hands into two fists. For a second I almost thought she was going to hit me. I wanted to reach out then and touch her, but I was afraid she might push me away. Then she looked off down the harbour.

We stood like that for a long time. Neither of us said a word. A pair of shrieking gulls flew overhead and cast a shadow down on us. Jack let out a loud raucous shriek of his own. He wanted those other birds to know that he was one of them and that he was very much alive.

Chapter Five

Things were pretty morose around my house. It was one of those bad breakfast scenes. Something wasn't going right for my old man.

"What is it, Dad?" I asked.

"I thought I was going to get a new job with the Regional Authority, but it fell through. They still won't touch me. They only want to hire people who will tell them what they want to hear."

"You don't want to work for those idiots anyway," my mother consoled him.

The stupid dump and the incinerator — it was part of our every day life. I couldn't get away from it.

"You're too good for them," I said.

He shook his head and stared into a spoonful of corn flakes like he was looking for an answer. Man, he looked pretty bummed out.

"It's not just the work. There's something else going on. They wouldn't tell me what. Heck, they wanted me out of there. It was stupid of me to think they'd hire me to do anything. They want consultants who are only going to tell them what they want to hear."

"What do they want to hear?" I asked. "That they're heroes, I suppose, for putting in an incinerator."

"It might get worse."

"What are you talking about?" my mom asked, pouring my father another cup of coffee.

He just shook his head.

The wind came up at about eleven. I rang Marina and she said she could get away. This would be a first for a lot of things for me: the first date I ever had where I'd meet the girl on my sailboard, and the first date I ever had with a girl at a dump. But this was one extraordinary girl.

I rigged the sail, eased off from land and tacked way over to the western shore before heading north and east to meet Marina at the halfway point where we had met before — the little stream that ran into the harbour.

She was already there with her board beached when I arrived.

I had on my flashy pink and turquoise wetsuit. "You look good," she said.

"Thanks. So do you." I wanted to say more. I wanted to tell her that her hair looked like a beautiful, red fire and that she had a smile that could light up a city, but I knew better than to move too fast.

"We need to know what we're up against," Marina said. "Let's check out this stream."

We could both smell the stench of something from the water, but today it didn't really look polluted. Marina had on a little red backpack and pulled out a couple of empty pop bottles. "We'll need a few samples."

"Hey, you sound like a professional."

"I don't exactly know what I'm doing, but I know that if we want to do any good we have to get the facts."

So we hiked up Bedford Brook to where it stopped in a little marshy pond. The high wall of dirt that acted as the outer barrier of the ash dump was just beyond it.

Marina cupped her hands in the water and rubbed her fingers together. "Feel this," she said.

"Sort of slimy. Look, if you put your head down low to the water so that it catches the light on the surface, you can see a thin film of something."

Marina saw it too. She pulled out a bottle and took a sample of the water near the surface. The water had the same foul odour as before, only stronger. "I guess I knew it was like this all along," I admitted to her. "I've been here a hundred times before. Sometimes it's just the stuff rotting in the marsh, though, that makes a film in the water like this. Swamp gas and stuff."

"Maybe. Maybe not."

We were both looking around at the little pond, looking for signs of something wrong. Our eyes both fixed on it at the same time. Floating in a little pool between two big boulders were some birds. Whatever kind they were, they were dead. Marina ran over to the spot. I followed behind her.

"Mergansers," I said. I was a big fan of these magical duck-like birds with the red tuft on the back of their heads. Here, still on the surface of the water, were a parent merganser and three little ones, maybe two months old. Marina immediately picked up one of the young ones. She looked it over carefully, almost clinically.

"No bullets. No teeth marks. Something killed them and it wasn't another animal."

I picked up the parent. Despite its lifeless appearance, it was still a beautiful bird. We had found what Marina was looking for: evidence. But I didn't think it could do any good. If we took the next step, we would be getting in deep, probably over our heads. I knew people wouldn't care enough about a couple of dead birds to want to make any real changes. But I had no choice.

Marina put the three dead young mergansers into her pack and I carried the big one. We circled around to the foot of the dirt barrier and looked for some obvious place where it was leaking something out. I couldn't see anything obvious.

"Maybe it comes up from the ground water underneath, after it's leaked out of the landfill," I said.

I was kind of hoping that Marina wasn't going to do this, but she did it anyway: she sprinted to the top of the landfill wall. I followed as best as I could.

On the other side of the mound was the pit where the ash from the incinerator was dumped. A guy in a big bulldozer was pushing some dirt over top of it. Hundreds of gulls swarmed and shrieked overhead. For a minute, I was sure that Marina was going to scream out something at the guy on the bulldozer.

Instead, she sat down and held one of the young birds up to her face. "I'm sorry," she said to it. "I'm sorry we did this to you."

I sat beside her and understood exactly what she was feeling. But I knew at that moment that I was the stronger one, the more logical one. I didn't want us to go down to the landfill office with the dead birds and yell and scream at the bastards like crazy kids.

"We take these birds someplace to be studied. We make their sacrifice worthwhile," I said.

"You mean like some government lab or something?"

"I don't trust the government. They approved this godforsaken thing. Even though my old man fought it. They wouldn't listen."

"Then you're saying there's nothing we can do?"

I saw the look on her face. The truth was that I didn't think anything would make a difference. I'd seen my old man go down the tubes trying to prove that the dump and the incinerator were wrong. Why bother? But I suddenly heard myself talking like him, like my father before he gave up. I knew what he would have done. "We're going to have to put up our own money and pay some independent lab to do it."

"I've got fifty bucks," she said.

"I've only got thirty. Together that should do it."

On the way back to our boards, I couldn't help but wish things were different. I really didn't want to get into some impossible battle. I wasn't the type to get involved in a cause. All I wanted was a chance to fall in love with this girl and for her to fall in love with me. I'd been so long without a girlfriend that I ached real bad inside.

And I really didn't want to fight what I knew would be a losing battle. "I have to warn you," I told Marina, "I come from a long line of losers."

I was thinking about my old man. And I was remembering my grandfather who'd lost his farm to a highway that got put through his land and then ended up so messed up that he drank himself to death.

"Funny you say that, because that's how I feel sometimes," Marina said. "That's why we'll work well together, though. A couple of losers know so much defeat that they'll do just about anything to win for once."

I smiled. No. I laughed. I couldn't believe I was laughing under the circumstances, but I was.

"You're good for me, you know that," I told her.

"I know," she said. "I'm very good for you."

Chapter Six

They want a hundred and twenty bucks to do the tests on the birds," Marina told me on the phone. She had already called around and found a place called Quality Labs about thirty kilometres away in Dalton. "We'll need another ten bucks for a courier."

"I can ride them there on my bike," I told her.

"It's okay. I already called. The courier is going to be here in twenty minutes."

"But the money . . . "

"That's okay, too. My father said he'd chip in. But you'll have to get over here with your part of the loot. The guy at the lab said he had to have the money up front. Cash. He knew he was dealing with a kid."

"I'm gonna have to bust it if I want to get over there in twenty minutes," I said. I was a little knocked out by the way Marina was so efficient. I mean, she didn't mess around. If it was just me, I probably would have just changed my mind about following through with tests for the poor mergansers, but not this lady.

"You have good legs," she said. "In fact, I think you have great legs. You can do it."

"I do?" I said, not knowing how to take this kind of compliment from a girl.

"Yes, stupid, you do. Now use them to get you over here with your money, buster. And by the way, my father wants you to bring along Jack."

So I was off on the road again. If nothing else, this business with Marina was going to keep me in good shape. Jack seemed to be quite happy to be in his little metal cage again, with the wind in his face. I had this kooky image of me being his wings. If he couldn't fly, then I could fly for him. I only wished I could do the same for the mergansers.

I always felt like I had as much right on the road as anybody in a car. I probably didn't stay close enough to the shoulder. And when I sailed down the road, I spaced out a little too much if there wasn't much traffic. So here I was on my way to see Marina for the second time that day. I was going to turn over my life savings to her to help find out what killed a couple of birds, when I already knew what had killed them. It was pretty obvious. But it wasn't enough to just say it was the crud from the landfill. We needed hard facts.

My mind was running through all this just as I was passing the side road that went down to the incinerator dump site. I loved the sound of my mountain bike tires gripping the hard pavement as I rolled along at top speed. Well, I suppose I wasn't paying attention when this garbage truck came hauling ass out onto the main road from the dump.

The idiot driving didn't stop at the stop sign. I guess he figured he didn't see any cars, so what was the point? He gunned the big diesel engine and pulled out in front of me. I had a split second to decide if I wanted to bail out or go splat into it. And then there was Jack to worry about.

These things happen pretty quick and it's funny how your mind actually goes into hyperdrive and sorts it all out to come up with a decision, sometimes right, sometimes wrong. I knew that if I tried to veer out of the way, I'd plow straight into the barbed wire fence surrounding the entrance to the landfill and I had never been friends with barbed wire. I also didn't feel like chewing the steel plates on the side of the truck.

So I grabbed onto Jack's cage with one hand, lifting it under my left arm. Then I found the loose stones of the gravel on the side of the road and threw the bike into a quick right turn and a slide. Still holding Jack with one hand and the handlebars with the other, I made a reasonably controlled wipe-out. My right leg took the worst of it as I laid the bike down and skidded along the gravel until we stopped.

Meanwhile, the truck had made its turn and was pumping ugly clouds of black exhaust out of its stack. The driver had never even seen me. He was on down the road grinding gears on his merry way. I simply wasn't a problem of his.

Jack was squawking at me now. He was probably thinking that human beings had some real strange habits. But he was okay. I had kept him from smashing down in the ground. I crawled out from under my bike and surveyed my ripped pants and the blood on my leg from where I'd scraped skin against stones. I stood up and yelled something real nasty at the truck driver who I'm sure never heard me above the roar of his engine.

The bike was okay. I was happy about that. The body would heal itself, but if I wrecked my bike it would have cost money to fix. And right now I was hurrying off to give all my hard-earned cash to Marina.

With my pride in really bad shape, I strapped Jack back onto my bike and rode off, pumping my bad leg as hard as my good leg and feeling an occasional drop of blood trickle down into my sock. I kept telling myself that this was like our second "date". Since I'd never gone out on what most guys would call a real date, I figured that this was as close as it was going to get. I'd heard other guys brag about making out with girls on their first or second date. And sometimes they'd brag about how much money they spent ahead of time to go out to dinner or a movie or whatever. I figured I had a good story for guys like Bickman and Grieg when I got back together with them. *I met this crazy girl named*

Marina, right? And, like, on our second date, I blew thirty bucks to have a couple of dead ducks dissected. Naw, somehow I didn't think those turkeys would be able to appreciate it.

I saw the Purolater truck sitting in Marina's driveway when I got there.

"Did you bring the money?" she asked me. No hi, no hello, nothing.

I handed over the loot. She put it in an envelope and sealed it up in the box that had, I figured, the dead birds and the water sample.

When the Purolater guy took off, Marina looked at my shredded pants and bloody leg. "What happened to you?" she asked.

"I had a slight disagreement with a Mack truck about who had the right of way."

"I won't ask who won," she said. "You okay?" There was more warmth in her voice now, more concern. She looked genuinely worried — this time about me.

I smiled, soaking in the attention. "Yeah, I'm okay. In fact, I feel like a million dollars."

She held out her hand. Jack and I followed her inside.

In the kitchen, she introduced me to her mom who had the same fiery red hair as Marina.

Mrs. Ryerson was a very pretty woman, but you could tell she'd had a rough time of it. I could read the whole story in her face and the soft, but painful way she smiled. It was the story of living with a husband that was not long for this world. And it was the story of someone who had lost in a big way. I kept thinking about what Marina had said about being a loser.

Maybe we were all losers. Maybe that's what attracted me to Marina. It's what we had in common.

"Are you as loonie as my daughter?" Mrs. Ryerson asked me.

"Excuse me?" I asked. I wasn't quite sure where she was coming from.

"No, Mom," Marina answered for me. "He's worse. Much worse. This is a guy who wears a pink and blue wetsuit, wrestles with garbage trucks in his spare time, and never goes anywhere without his one-winged seagull."

Mrs. Ryerson looked at Jack and me and shook her head.

I turned to Marina. "I thought you asked me to bring him along."

She bopped me on the arm. "I did. I was just teasing."

Jack let out one of his ear-piercing screams just to get in on the conversation.

"Does he have to be in here?" Mrs. Ryerson asked.

"Is that Jack?" I heard the feeble voice of her father say from the other room.

"Yes, sir," I said. "I'll take him back outside."

"No, no. Don't. I asked Marina to ask you to bring him. Bring him in, please."

I took Jack in to Marina's father who was still sitting in the same Lazy Boy. He clicked off the TV with the remote.

"Set him here," he said.

I put Jack's cage down on the table beside the chair. "He's still pretty mean," I said. "Be careful."

I still had wounds that were healing from Jack's razor sharp beak. We had a pretty awkward relationship. He ate food out of my hand but would have been just as happy to swallow a couple of my fingers if he could rip them off my hand.

"We'll be okay," Mr. Ryerson said. "You kids go have fun."

"You're sure?" I asked, watching Mr. Ryerson studying Jack's injured wing. I was also worried that Jack would likely do what was natural for him and do some damage to the furniture. But Marina's father was waving us away.

In the kitchen, Mrs. Ryerson kindly moved on to another room and we were left alone in the afternoon sunshine.

Go have fun, her father had said. Fun wasn't exactly the word I could use to describe being with Marina. She was always pretty serious. Even there in her kitchen, we looked at each other but didn't quite know what to say. When I felt another drop of blood trickle out of my leg and dribble into my sock, I guess I automatically looked down.

"Oh, I'm sorry," she said. "Let me fix you up."

She took a warm washcloth and began to dab at the scrape. It hurt, I think, but I was too dizzy with the fact that she was touching me to worry about pain. She was very gentle and caring, and I realized that this was the other side of her personality.

When she sat back down, I asked her something that had been bugging me. "Did you leave behind a boyfriend back where you came from?"

"The guys were all jerks," she said. "They were all hopeless."

"But you must have gone out with some of them." After all, this was our second date. I wanted some background info. "I can't imagine that a girl who . . . well . . . looks like you didn't have guys tripping all over each other to go out with you."

She laughed at the compliment but shook it off. "Oh, they'd ask me out. But they hated it when I wanted to talk about anything serious. It turned them right off. Eventually they just stopped asking. I bored them."

"I could never think of you as boring."

"I guess I could say the same about you," she countered.

"Do we know what we're getting into?" I asked her. I really meant the business with the lab and the landfill leak, but I think I wanted my question to have a double meaning.

"No," she answered. "Do you think we know what we're getting into?"

"No," I said.

"Do you think we should give it up?" This time maybe it was her question that had the double meaning.

"No way," I told her.

We sat for a long time after that and didn't talk, but it was strange because I didn't feel uncomfortable about it at all. When I went in to pick up Jack for the trip home, I saw a really weird sight. Mr. Ryerson had Jack out of his cage and was holding the bird in the crook of his arm. Marina's father looked half asleep, but one hand was gently stroking the bird. Jack seemed perfectly content. This from a bird whose greatest joy in life seemed to be trying to dismember the guy who fed him his favourite fish scraps.

We stood there looking at her father and the bird, not saying anything. Then Marina whispered, "Could we keep Jack here? I'll build him a big pen outside."

"Sure," I said. "If you don't think he'll be any trouble."

"No trouble at all," Marina answered.

Chapter Seven

I didn't know what good it would do to prove that those birds had been poisoned. Remember, I'd watched my father try to persuade the Regional Authority that putting a landfill near the harbour was a bad idea. And he was a professional, an expert. My father, the environmental engineer. Well, in the end it didn't matter a gnat's hair whether he was right or wrong. They went ahead and did what they thought was the cheapest and easiest way to get rid of the garbage. The same thing happened all over again with the incinerator.

When I got home that night, my mom and dad were in the middle of a real blow-up fight. The subject was the usual: money. We were pretty broke. The magazine writing my father did was slim pickings and my mom was working part-time sixty kilometres away at the K-Mart. I walked into the house at the wrong time. I made a futile attempt to mumble a hello and slink off to my room.

"Damn it, Chris! You're old enough. Why don't you get some sort of summer job? There must be something out there. You can't just go chasing after girls and wasting your time goofing off on your windsurfer all summer."

"Right, Dad," I said. I didn't really want to deal with him. He usually wasn't like this. It was pretty sad to see how he'd gone downhill in the last few years. He used to be so full of energy and enthusiasm. Now he just worried about money and hassled Mom and me.

It was a good thing he didn't know I just gave my thirty bucks to Marina. "I'll go up to the Shell station and see if they need anybody to pump gas or change tires," I said. But it wasn't something I really wanted to do. Maybe I was being unfair to my family, but I knew I was in the middle of something important. I was in over my head but I was in it with Marina. I didn't want to waste my summer pumping gas.

"That's not going to make much difference," my mother said. She and my old man had been scrapping for too long for her to back down now.

"Look, right now we have to think about putting food on the table and paying the taxes. Everything will help. He should sell his bloody toy sailboat as well."

"Dad," I said, "I'm not going to sell my sailboard."

"Just take it easy, Chris," my mom said. She could see that I was ready to jump into the battle. She noticed my leg. "What happened?"

"Fell off my bike," I said.

"And wrecked a perfectly good pair of pants!" my old man shouted at me.

"I'm going to my room," I said, frustrated. It had been a monster of a day. My life was like an emotional roller-coaster this summer.

If it had been like old times, I could have sat down and talked about the mergansers with my parents. But I knew that if I even mentioned it, he'd get depressed and not want to talk about it. We losers were like that. So, as I walked off, I had a thousand unanswered questions in my head.

I lay on my bed listening to music with the earphones on: Nirvana, Mud Puppy, Enter

Reality and Good Idea Gone Bad. The good
stuff. I liked it loud and liked it hard. To be
honest, it kind of relaxed me. When I saw my
digital clock pop up on 11:30 I was still wide
awake. My dad and mom were asleep. They
had stopped arguing after a while and I think
they made up. In the big picture, though, I
knew that things were getting worse in my
family. I had to do something to make sense of
it all.

I got up off the bed and walked down past
the kitchen to my father's little cubby-hole
office. Feeling a little bit like a criminal, I clicked
on the light and looked at his filing cabinet. This
was my old man's personal territory. This was
his stuff and I knew I had no right to go digging
around here. But I needed more information, I
knew that. And I just couldn't bring myself to
talk to him about it, to get him involved. His
battle against the dump and the incinerator had
really messed him up. This was my fight. He
didn't have to be involved.

It was a good thing my old man was pretty
well organized — not like me at all. I thumbed
through his files until I came to *Incinerator*

right where it should have been, after *Hydro-electricity*.

It was a big fat file full of photocopies of research reports and magazine articles. Pretty tough reading, but my father had meticulous notes all over the place. Good old Dad. All the important points were underlined in red. I even found the notes he used for his presentation to the Regional Authority.

Incinerators in other parts of North America had been blamed for asthma in kids, I read, for depleting the ozone levels, for acid rain increases, and worse things. Parents had sued incinerator operators and landfills for illness and even death of not just animals but people. But in almost every court case, it was just too hard to pin down the fault and to make it stick. Lawyers could argue that it could be "any number of things in the environment" that cause the death of fish, ducks, or children. Apparently there were a number of different kinds of burners. Some just burned ordinary garbage. Others burned chemical waste. It all sounded pretty scary. Included with the papers were the actual specs on the incinerator that was to be built.

I made some notes for myself about the "potential toxicity of incinerator fly ash". It was a list of chemicals that would be left behind from burning ordinary trash: mercury, lead, cadmium, copper, chromium, and dioxin. Then I hit on a letter. It was from my father to the Regional Authority director. Part of it read:

Based on my research, I strongly advise against the incinerator route for reducing landfill disposal. The incinerator configuration you propose to install is using technology that is at least 15 years old. Not only will it increase excessive amounts of carbon monoxide and carbon dioxide, but also particulate discharge laced with dioxin that will come down locally and at sea. Also, the resulting fly ash you propose to "filter" from such an incinerator will be far more concentrated in toxic substances (list attached) than simple landfill refuse and you propose no really safe means for disposal of such ash as will be left on site in the same manner as other common refuse. The clay liner is not designed to contain such substances — or at least has not been tested for effectiveness.

It is imperative that other alternatives are explored. Please feel free to consult with me and my colleagues in the Department of the Environment on these and other issues for which we will make ourselves readily available.

Yours truly,
Steven Knox, environmental consultant

Stapled to this letter, however, was another one, this one from my dad's former boss at Environment.

Dear Steve,

I regret to inform you that your contract with us will be terminated at the end of the month. Monies are getting tighter and we are being forced to reduce our staff, particularly those on short-term renewable contracts, like yourself. We appreciate all your fine work with us and trust you will find gainful employment elsewhere.

Yours,
Clyde Rollins, Executive Director

But I knew that it wasn't just the cutbacks that got my father canned. And he knew it too. He had been the only one "let go". He was also the only one in his department to speak out against the incinerator.

Somebody was at the door now. I tried to close the file but the papers fell out on the floor.

It was my mom. "Chris, what on earth are you doing here?" She looked really shocked.

I was still hanging on to Dad's letter of dismissal. Mom came over and looked at it.

"I just felt like I needed a few answers," I said.

Her surprise had given way to anger. "You have no right to be doing this! You should have asked your father's permission first."

I didn't know what to say. She was right, of course, but she probably knew why I hadn't asked. "I found this," I said, feeling more than a little guilty but hoping that the letter would somehow explain why I couldn't get Dad directly involved.

"That's all a long time ago. It's all over with. No point in getting back into it. And there's no excuse for you to be in here going through your father's papers."

I started to pick up the papers that had fallen to the floor. I couldn't win. Nothing I tried to do was going to help anybody. She must have seen my look of defeat because she suddenly changed. "Here, let me help clean this up," she said, her voice much softer.

"It's not over, Mom," I said.

She shook her head and smiled. "Pretty soon something good will happen for us. Things will be different." She bent down and helped me pick up all the papers I'd spilled. She handed them back to me.

"Don't tell Dad I was rooting in his stuff, okay? I didn't mean any harm."

"I know you didn't," she said.

I looked at the papers I was holding onto. "I was having a hard time sleeping. But this will work the trick. Nothing like a fat technical report to put a guy to sleep." My mom didn't say another word as I walked off towards my room with the file under my arm. The next day I would photocopy what I needed and return everything. I still felt like a criminal, but at least I was a criminal with a worthy cause.

Chapter Eight

The only work Bud Gilfoy had for me was three hours a morning pumping gas. I took it, knowing it would make my old man happy. The Shell station was only about a couple of kilometres from where Marina lived as well. That was the clincher. It was a dumb job, working around gasoline fumes and airheads. But it would mean a few more bucks to keep my family off welfare.

Friday morning, I was putting twenty bucks of high test into somebody's big Mercury when Marina walked down the road. The other guys around the station started to give her the eye and couldn't believe it when she walked up to me.

"We have to talk," she said. She had an envelope in her hand.

I wasn't paying attention and the Merc's tank must have been full. The automatic switch on the pump handle didn't stop when the tank was full, and gasoline began to squirt out onto the ground.

"Pay attention, kid!" the guy in the car yelled at me. I grabbed the handle and clicked it off.

"Sorry," I said.

"You don't expect me to pay for what you spilled, do you?"

"No," I said. The pump read $20.80.

"Just give me twenty," I said.

"Here," he said, handing me a ten and a five. "And consider yourself lucky that I didn't complain to your boss." He started his big engine, and squealed some rubber on his way out of there. I knew I'd have to cover the rest of what he didn't pay out of my own pocket.

"Sorry," Marina said.

The guys inside the station were pointing at me and having a good long laugh at my expense.

"Don't worry about it. Let me see what you have."

She opened the envelope and handed me the lab report.

"I'm not sure I understand," I said, trying to make sense of it. There were some numbers indicating levels of various chemicals.

"Read the bottom."

I read aloud: " 'All four test birds had extraordinary high levels of chromium, lead and mercury. Such metals do not normally exist in the natural environment locally at these concentrations. Other toxic substances are present in the water sample as well, we believe, but this would require further tests. Our fee schedule is attached.' We've got evidence then?" I asked.

"A guy from the lab called me today and asked me to tell him where we found the birds. He said it should be reported to the Department of Health."

"And? . . . "

"I didn't tell him."

"Why?"

"I remember my father trying to prove that his sickness was brought on by working around benzine at the chemical plant. He had his doctors take every test possible. Then he made the results available to anyone who wanted to examine them: the safety regulators, the company, the lawyers. And they figured a way to use it against him. I don't think I can trust anyone."

I was afraid for a minute she meant me too.

She could read me like a book. "I didn't mean you, stupid."

Barry Grieg pulled up just then in his four by four, jacked up, macho-man truck. He gave Marina the once-over and I wanted to clobber him, but then he turned to me. "Fill it, please, Crissy," he said, using the name locals had called me when I was a little kid and my parents had let my hair grow real long.

When my shift ended at noon, Marina made two copies of the lab report on the photocopier at the drugstore and stuffed them in my back pocket. She had a kind of fire in her eyes.

"What?" I asked. I desperately needed to know what she was thinking.

"I want us to forget about the proper channels right now. I just want to go there to the incinerator site and rub their noses in it. I want those bastards to know that we have evidence."

"That's crazy. It won't do any good." I couldn't believe the nerve of this girl.

Marina looked at me like I had just turned into her worst enemy. And all at once I realized what I had just said had sounded so much like my father's words. She reached in my back pocket for the copies of the report.

"Wait!" I grabbed her hand. "You're right," I lied. "Let's do it."

Marina and I then asked Mrs. Grandy, who was headed home from shopping, for a ride. She had to go down past the landfill site and I was so syrupy polite in asking for a ride that she couldn't possibly turn us down.

When she dropped us off at the gate, Marina was laughing. "Chris, you're a real charmer when you want to be. That lady thinks you're the sweetest thing since sugar was invented."

"I know how to use my charms if I have to," I told her. But I was already thinking of the task ahead. Of all the years that I'd lived with the bloody landfill incinerator project, this was the first time that I was going to go in the front gate, go up to the incinerator office, and talk to Ron Gibson, the supervisor. Right then, I guess Marina was feeling pretty powerful in her cause. It wasn't the logical thing to do but I didn't have the heart to talk her out of it. "You're sure this is the route to go?" I asked Marina.

"No. But I want to try the direct approach first."

Looking down the roadway to the entrance, however, I spotted the checkpoint. There was a guard there who kept track of every truck that came through and would stop anyone who didn't have a permit or a reason to be there. I had a feeling that this would include us.

"Let's save the direct approach for when we're inside," I told her.

We walked a little ways down the road until we found a comfortable gap in the barbed wire. I gently lifted it and made room for Marina to crawl through.

It was plenty easy skirting the guard shed, but when we got to the building that sat beside the incinerator itself I was starting to have second thoughts.

"They could have us arrested for trespassing," I said.

"It should be the other way around. We should have them arrested."

The incinerator was billowing that white grey plume up over our heads, but it was so far up, so far away, that it didn't seem real. At the base of the stack was a dingy mud-brown concrete block of a windowless building. Inside was the fire. A crazy mix of sound filled the air — the bulldozers out in the dump, the roar of the flames inside, and the sound of the steam-powered turbine that was producing electricity. I knew that one of the reasons this thing came into being was the fact that the burning trash could be used to boil water, make steam, and produce power. On the surface it sounded like a great idea: burn trash to make electricity. But it wasn't that simple.

At the far end, away from the stack, was the main door. Cars were parked outside, each covered in a film of dust. I took Marina's hand and together we made our way towards our confrontation.

I was a bit shocked at first when I opened the door and discovered the inside looked quite ordinary — like it was a dentist's office or something.

A woman was sitting at a computer terminal, typing. She looked quite puzzled as we walked in. You could tell she wasn't used to getting too many uninvited visitors.

"We'd like to see Mr. Gibson, please," I said politely but firmly.

She looked even more puzzled. "Does he know you're coming?"

"Not exactly," Marina said. "But it's important."

"I don't know," the lady said. I could tell that she didn't know what to do with us but was probably too polite to just tell us to get lost.

Just then another door opened.

"What's up, Vivian?" Gibson asked when he saw Marina and me.

"I don't know, Mr. Gibson. These two young people just sort of showed up. They say they want to speak to you . . . "

Gibson was a big guy, maybe six-two. He was mostly bald but covered the top of his head with what was left of his hair on the sides swept over the shiny spot. He had the no-nonsense look that I'd seen on school principals. Something about him made me sweat, something about being here inside this ugly building that I'd stared at and hated for so many years.

Gibson looked us over. "If you're looking for summer work, I'm sorry. We don't hire students."

"It's not that," Marina told him. "We need to talk to you."

My guess is that it was because Marina was so good-looking. Gibson couldn't quite bring himself to kick us out the door. "Come on in and tell me what's on your mind," he said.

We followed him into his office which looked pretty rich. "Have a seat," he said.

I knew that once we got here it would be Marina, not me, to make the first move. "We don't think this place is safe," she said flat out. "The incinerator is producing poisonous gases, and the ash that's left over is poisonous as well."

Gibson looked at her like she had just spoken to him in Russian. He blinked. "You want to run that past me one more time?" he said.

I knew that he had heard her perfectly well. "Let's be more specific," I said trying to keep my cool. I could already see a kind self-righteous defensiveness setting in with Gibson.

"Fine," he said. "Let's get specific," he repeated, mocking me.

"Your ash has high levels of heavy metals as well as other deadly stuff. You dump it out there in the ground and it's getting into the ground water. It's killing animals and it's probably running into the harbour where it's doing more damage."

I unfolded one of the photocopies of the lab report and slid it across his big, fancy mahogany desk. He picked it up and studied it.

Gibson wrinkled his brow and studied the paper. "You two have been reading too much Greenpeace propaganda," he said trying to brush us off. But I didn't react. "Oh, I get it. This is a joke, right? You're doing this on a dare?"

I wished I had the dead mergansers right then to stick in front of his nose and show him just how real it was. Or better yet, I wished that I had brought along Jack, another victim of a different sort, to lunge at this Gibson character and pluck his eyes out.

"No joke. No dare," Marina said. "We have evidence that this place isn't safe. You're leaking toxic waste into the water outside the landfill and you're pumping death into the sky. And we want to close this place down."

Whew. Marina had a pretty straightforward way of making a point.

"Get out of here!" Gibson stood up suddenly. "You have no right to come in here with crazy accusations. Now get the hell out of here! Or would you rather I call the cops?"

Chapter Nine

In truth, it felt pretty neat sitting in the back of the police cruiser with Marina, separated from the cop driving us by a big slab of bulletproof glass. I mean, I kind of liked the idea of getting in trouble for something that was a worthy cause. I knew that our parents would understand.

The cop thought we were just a couple of goofy kids. He said, "Look, I don't know what you were up to. But Gibson didn't press charges. You were lucky. Just don't go back."

Marina tried to explain about the dead mergansers, about the heavy metals, but the cop waved his hand in the air. "You kids watch too much TV," he said, which was pretty funny because Marina and I watched almost no TV.

Marina got dropped off first. The policeman told her mother what it was all about.

She looked at me still sitting like a prisoner in the back of the car. She must have thought it was all my fault. I could hear her say to the cop, "She's never been in any trouble before. Ever."

And suddenly I got worried that we had screwed up, that her parents might not let her see me again. This got me pretty worried.

Dad didn't act the way I expected he would act either. He stood silently while the officer recounted our crime. "Get in the house," was all my dad said to me.

Inside, he sat me down in his little office. He was wringing his hands. I could tell he was upset and mad but trying to control himself. "I thought I told you to stay away from that place."

"You did. But I had a good reason. They've got a leak. It's getting into the ground water and killing birds." I handed him a copy of the lab report.

My father didn't take it right away. He seemed confused. Then he took a deep breath and looked me straight in the eye. He took the report, scanned it, then looked at me. "You showed this to Gibson?"

"Yeah, Marina and me."

"And he threw you out on your butts?"

"He called in the police."

"You're lucky he didn't have you locked up."

"So what do you think I should do next?"

My father looked away from me and out the window at the sparrows in his bird-feeder. He didn't say anything at all. Then my mother came into the room and sat down on the desk beside him.

"I think now is as good a time as any to discuss it," she said to my dad.

I didn't know what *it* was. "Discuss what?" I asked.

My father sucked in a gulp of air and scratched his arm. He was just about to say something but couldn't seem to get it out.

Instead, Mom did it for him. "Chris, your father and I have decided that we should move."

"What?" I shouted, jumping up out of my chair.

"There's no work for me here, Chris. And nobody in the Department of the Environment or any other government agency is going to give me a job. When I stood up against the dump site years ago, they got worried. They tolerated me when I protested the dump in the first place, then the expansion. But when I made a case against including an incinerator, they all decided I was out of the club. It's lousy, but that's the way it is. Time to cut my losses and leave."

"Yeah, but it's not just you."

"Your father thinks there's a better chance out west. More opportunity. It will be a gamble but there's no reason for us to stay here."

"I love it here!" I found myself shouting back. But I have to admit: right then I wasn't thinking about the land or the harbour. I was thinking about Marina.

My mother seemed pretty uncomfortable and what came out next didn't sound all that convincing. "You'll learn to love it out there. Maybe we can move some place with mountains."

"Big deal."

"Be reasonable," my father said, trying to sound very cool about everything. "I mean, look what's happened to us ever since the landfill went in. Look at you today, coming home with a police escort. We have to get away from here."

I think that, for the first since I was twelve years old, I wanted to hit my old man just then.

I wanted to hit him hard and knock him down on the floor. Here I had just made one of the biggest moves of my life — Marina and I had gone to confront Gibson, to make a stand against the system — and now my father was telling us it was time to tuck our tails between our legs and run away. What a bunch of losers!

"I'm not going," I said.

I got up to leave the room. I was going to go for a walk in the woods, but my mom grabbed me by the arm. "Please, Chris. There's more."

What *more* could there be. My old man squirmed uncomfortably in his chair.

"Remember I made a bid on that new consulting work for the Department of the Environment?"

"Yeah, you were never given a chance. I know that."

"I was stupid to expect they'd forgive me for bucking the system in the past."

"So what's that have to do with this? You didn't really think you'd get it. You said so."

"Right. But I didn't even know what I was applying for. The specs were pretty vague. But I talked with some of my old colleagues this week. And what I found out has a lot to do with why we're moving."

I looked at my mother. She was in on this. Whatever it was, she already knew.

"The Regional Authority," Dad said, looking away from me now and back out at the bird-feeder, "had applied for permission to put in a second burner — another incinerator. They want to burn chemical waste from factories that can't dispose of their crud in any other way."

"But they can't do that!" I shouted again. "They'll screw up the same way with another incinerator, only this time it will be worse. It really sucks!"

"It's chemical suicide for the air, and for the harbour. We'd be crazy to stay living here," he said.

"But it doesn't make any sense," I said. "Marina and I have *evidence* that they can't even deal safely with the ash from the incinerator now. We've got lab reports on four dead mergansers to prove it. You saw for yourself."

"Chris, you don't have to persuade me. But Environment has already given them the go-ahead. They had a consulting report saying it will be safe. It was a set up. But the facts don't matter. It will mean big money for the Regional Authority. It will mean more jobs. And that report is all they needed. They even claim the clay liner in the dump is capable of containing any contaminant from the ash."

"But that's not true. Anybody with eyes could go there and see what a disaster the place is."

"But most people don't go there," my mom said. "Most people never see the landfill or the incinerator. The people who make decisions just see reports and they assume that reports are factual."

"I've read hundreds of these studies, Chris. A good bullshitter can make black look like white and white look like Agent Orange."

"So we expose it for what it is. We tell everybody the truth."

"You're forgetting," Mom said. "Everybody who cared — most people who fought the landfill anyway — has already gone. We should have left too. We just didn't have anywhere to go to."

"There's big money in it for the Regional Authority. They get paid handsomely for dispos-ing of what nobody else will touch. Some people around here will think this could turn into a really big money-making industry."

"But there must be laws. Something that could stop this."

"Yes and no," Dad said. "There are enough loopholes that this project can go through. And soon. There's just not enough local opposition. The Regional Authority already has signed a deal with Dial Chemical. They plan on shipping the stuff by barge down river and along the coast, then up the harbour to the site. I guess they're going to use the old government fishing wharf that's been sitting there wasting away. From what I hear, they're going to start stock-piling the waste there on site even before the second stack is built. It's all going to happen pretty quickly."

It was too much for me all at once. The name of Dial Chemical rang like a gunshot through my head. That was the company Marina's father had worked for. I hung my head and found myself squeezing my palms against my fore-head. My mom put an arm around me. "We're sorry, Chris. We know you care. And we know what you were trying to do today. It's just too late. It's time to move."

But while my parents were already packed and gone in their mind, I was still dead centre *here* in my home. I wasn't ready to give up.

My father gave my lab report back to me with that all too familiar look of defeat. "Heavy metals might only be the beginning," he said. "Dioxin, PCBs. Stuff that we haven't even begun to do research on. And you'd better know this," he said, pointing to the lab report. "The company that did the new assessment for importing waste was Quality Research Limited. The guys who work at Quality Labs, the ones who tested your birds, they're all part of the same organization. By now Gibson will have been on the horn to them. Don't be too surprised if they're not too helpful to you from here on."

Chapter Ten

I went for a walk along the shoreline after that and watched the sun go down over the harbour. I couldn't bring myself to call Marina. It was good that my old man had put everything on the table. He was forty years old and had grown tired and cynical. Maybe I'd be that way when I was his age. My mom had always been supportive of his battles before. She'd always been behind me, too, in whatever I wanted to do — the windsurfing, the wounded animals I'd brought home. They were both good parents. But now they wanted to cut their losses and split. The more I thought about it the less angry I was at them. In fact, their logic was correct. Why stay on to fight a losing battle and ruin your life?

If it hadn't been for Marina, I know I would have been ready to throw in the towel as well.

I watched the beauty of the red sky playing on the surface of the water. I felt the warm air on my face and took a big breath. The wind had come from a direction that left it clean and pure — or so I imagined. I don't guess that there is anywhere on earth that the air is completely natural. I knew that the planet was in reality a small place, a closed container.

On the surface, it seemed like there were good guys and bad guys. Polluters and environmentalists. But I knew it wasn't that simple. Dial Chemical made chemicals used in the manufacture of plastics. Plastics were in everything — cars, TVs, radios, bicycle parts, and sailboards. I was in there with everybody else. Let him who is without sin cast the first stone.

But that didn't mean we all had to sit back and watch a beautiful place like Rocky Harbour be turned into a hellhole.

I went to bed that night confused, real confused. I didn't talk to my parents any more about it. I didn't call Marina. I just wanted to sleep. I wanted escape.

And when I woke up the next morning, I did a pretty weird thing. I dressed in my work clothes, I ate some Cheerios, drank two glasses of orange juice, and pedalled all the way to the Shell station where I went to work as if nothing had happened.

I pumped gas, put some air in a couple of tires, and checked the oil level in a Toyota Camry and a Dodge Aries. And I decided that for the afternoon, I'd go home and get on my board for a sail. A ripping southwest wind was up on the harbour.

"Marina called," my mom said when I got home for a late lunch.

"Thanks, Mom," I said and wolfed down three serious soyaburgers — her specialty.

"Your father went to the realtor to put the house on the market," she said to me.

I stopped chewing and looked at her just then, but she turned away from me. What could I say? My father was selling our home out from under us. "That's nice," I said, trying to show no emotion at all.

I finished eating, threw my plate in the dirty water in the sink and grabbed my wetsuit. I started for the door and then stopped. I knew my mom was hurting and I didn't know what to do for her. But I put my arms around her and gave her a hug. "Things will turn out," I said.

Right then I was feeling no pain, no loss, no confusion. It was a thing guys could do, I understood that. When life got too complicated, I could just shut everything off. I could go to work. I could go sailing.

"Chris, be careful out there. Don't take any chances."

"Don't worry, Mom, I'll be okay. I always come back in one piece, right?"

She smiled but I knew she still worried about me every time I went out windsurfing alone.

I looked to the far shore, kicked my board out into the shallow water, set a course for the northwest to tack on the wind and I was off. I felt the cold, clean air pumping into my lungs, the strain on my right arm, the tension on the harness as I scudded along, barely touching down on water. I didn't look north and east to see the incinerator stack. I would pretend it wasn't there. When I came in close to the far shore — in record time I might add — I refused to give myself time to rest. I wanted to push it. I wanted to go home with aching, sore muscles. I was in my radical mode and just as I was about to crash into a big rock, I snapped a full speed jibe, only to have the sail whip around, out of my control. The boom caught me square in the nose and sent me sprawling into the water. I came up sputtering and angry. Nothing was broken; the boom, after all, was only light aluminum tubing, but I cursed my board and cursed my bad luck.

I lay in the water under the canopy of the dacron sail feeling a little sorry for myself. But I also felt cocooned and cut off from the world. I caught my breath, got my bearings without even looking up, just feeling the wind suck under the sail. As I curled my feet up into the straps I felt the lift, and I was on the move again.

This time I was headed straight out the harbour mouth and out to sea. The water was deep and scary and I could feel the strange tug of a strong current under me. I'd only been out this far once before, and I again found it hard to adjust to playing the shifting wind and the outpouring harbour current together. I was only slightly more cautious now, but once I had passed the tip of the land and felt the full-on brunt of the sea wind, I knew I had found what I was looking for.

Not far around the point was a sand bar. Waves a metre and a half high were breaking there. I'd seen one or two people on surfboards actually surf these waves before, but as far as I knew no one had ever tried to get any aerial manoeuvres on a sailboard here before.

But I had seen people on *Wide World of Sports* ride waves, using both wave and wind to perform magical feats of the impossible. And I was tired of the world of hope and failure, tired of the dead weight of living with worries about a stupid dump and poisons leaking everywhere. A wave was a thing of beauty, a thing to get in touch with, to match in wits and speed. It was something to make you free.

My adrenalin was pumping as I came up close to the cracking waves. There was a little teasing metre-high one about to break right in front of me, and I leaned my weight back, got the nose of the board in the air, and shot up the face of it just as it was breaking. I could feel the power, the surge of the white water as it washed over my legs but my sail had the full energy of the wind as it billowed and pulled me right up over top. I liked the rush of it all as I pulled in on the sail and settled back down lightly on the water, only to find myself driving up an even steeper wall of water with no time to think. I hauled in on the boom and shot upwards again, this time getting true air time and feeling as light-headed as the sea wind itself.

I raced farther out to sea, made a careful jibe and came about, giving serious thought as to how I would do this. I saw a dark hump on the horizon and tracked it carefully with my un-trained eye. This was not my element. The sea was a turbulent and unforgiving place. If I wiped out here, I might have a tough time getting back up on my board as waves tried to swamp me. A windsurfer sail can weigh next to nothing on dry land but if it's full of a few hundred litres of sea water it might as well be a tonne of lead.

I played the wind, spilling it to avoid getting too far ahead of this wave I had selected. It was bigger than the others, maybe up to my chin. It rolled and grew steeper as it approached the sand bar. Before I was ready for it, the wave had reached me. We were moving along at the same speed. The wind was in my favour. I dropped down the face of the wave and used my fin to make a bottom turn. Now I was sliding across the face of the wave at lightning speed. If I lost it now, I'd be chewing aluminum and fibreglass, I knew that. But the danger made it feel that much better. This was the kick I needed.

The wave was a long and perfectly peeling wall. For a loser, I realized that I, for once, was having some crazy luck for a first time wave/windsurfer. The wall was holding, the wind was with me and the world was frozen into the explosive, shimmering moment of wild abandon.

And then my luck ran out. I could see that the wave was now starting to collapse in front of me as well as behind. For a split second I wished that I had researched this sort of thing more carefully. Where was the handbook when you needed it? But no time for that. I could kick down and fight the white water, maybe get out in front of it, and stay dry. Then I would simply head for shore and a nice easy way out.

Or I could go the other route. The wave was nearly over my head now as it was about to collapse. I could carve a bottom turn and head straight up to the sky. Not much time to take a vote on it. What the hell, I figured.

I pulled in on the boom again, felt the immediate power of the wind and rocketed straight up the wall of the wave. I cracked through the upper lip just as the wave closed out. Both ends of the collapsing wall had met on top of me at the split second I made for lift-off.

I had never felt anything quite like it in my life. It was like two giant hands clapping together on both sides of me, trying to crush me in their wet maws, but I held on tight. I had speed and wind. Even the force of the collapsing wave itself had helped to generate this extraordinary leap to freedom. And as the sea smashed itself together in frothing salt spit, thunder, and confusion, I found myself tracking skyward. My sail was like a brilliant powerful wing pulling me up and away from the danger. I could see above the waves. I could see down the coast, and I thought for a brief instant I would keep going up and make company with the clouds.

Instead, the sail acted as a kindly parachute to bring me back to earth, and I made a beautiful splash as I hit the Atlantic. The wind didn't give me a chance to rest but pushed into my sail, sending me sliding over top of the incoming swells. No need to break the magic with another attempt, I told myself. The harbour mouth was ahead. Time to turn inland. Time to get back to the real world, no matter how screwed up it was.

By the time I came ashore I was thinking about my father's file concerning the incinerator. It was still sitting in my room. I'd read it all the way through but didn't understand everything. I had become caught up in other things and almost forgotten about it. Back in the house, I pulled out the pages that were most important. It was time for Marina to read them. That meant another bike ride to the drugstore and a long session popping change into the photocopier. It was getting late and I was tired, so I decided I shouldn't go over to her place just then. Instead, I pedalled back home. I was also feeling guilty again about holding onto the "borrowed" file. I wanted to sneak it back into my old man's office before he realized it was missing.

Chapter Eleven

When I got home I was shocked to see Marina waiting for me.

"I've been trying to get hold of you," she said.

I saw the car parked in the driveway. Her mom was pushing her father in a wheelchair. They were talking to my parents.

"What's going on?" I asked.

"My mom was mad at you at first. She thought it was you who got me into trouble, but I convinced her it was the other way around. It was different with my father. He likes you. In his eyes, you can do no wrong. In fact, he got back on the phone to the lab to ask for some more information. It was good to see him wanting to get involved. I think you've been a good influence on him."

"Me?" I asked.

"Yeah, I had you figured all wrong from the start. First impressions don't always hold up."

"I'm glad," I said, and I handed her the pages of the report I had copied. "Take a look at this when you get home. I have a feeling that some of this might come in handy sometime soon."

All of the adults were headed our way now. I stashed my papers inside my jacket and Marina put her copies into the back seat of their car. It was going to be one of those weird scenes with Marina's parents and my parents all together and everybody trying to be dopey polite.

I could see now that Mr. Ryerson was carrying Jack. He had on a pair of heavy gloves and was holding Jack in his lap. The guy still looked pretty awful. His skin had a pale white colour to it and he seemed to be having a hard time breathing. I knew that whatever it was that brought him here must have been a pretty big deal.

My own parents stayed in the background as Marina's mom rolled Mr. Ryerson up to me. I noticed his eyes first. For now the pain seemed to be gone. There was a kind of fire there, a spark that I hadn't seen before.

"Chris, I hope you don't mind this, but I got to thinking about ol' Jack here. He and I have become pretty good friends in the past few days. Not that he's always easy to get along with, mind you, but I respect that. He's a wild creature."

"Chris is always bringing home some poor injured animal ever since I can remember," Mom said, trying to make small talk.

Mrs. Ryerson smiled at her. "Always some poor thing out there in need of help."

Mr. Ryerson wasn't paying any attention to their talk. "Grab these other gloves here in my chair," he told me. I put them on and he handed Jack to me to hold. The first thing Jack did was take a big powerful bite into the glove, but I held onto him.

Then Mr. Ryerson reached into a bag on the side of his wheelchair and brought out a box. He opened the box and pulled out this strange mechanical contraption. He held it up in front of him, waiting for me to clue in.

"You were the one to find Jack. I didn't want to do this without your permission. But I thought about this day and night. I studied what was left of the stump of Jack's wing. Not much, but he still seems to have muscular control. So I made this."

I couldn't make head or tail of it. Straps, thin aluminum tubes hinged together, and a piece of dacron that looked like it had come off a windsurfer sail. I looked at Marina. She had a great big grin on her face. "It's a wing," Marina said.

My parents looked at each other like they had just discovered they were in the midst of a bunch of lunatics.

"I think I was wrong about a bird being able to live on the water without being able to fly," Mr. Ryerson said. "So I made this. It's a long shot. It might not work. Or if it works, Jack could get hurt. It was just an idea. But now it's up to you."

I didn't quite know what to say.

"I've made a padded fitting here so it will go over the stump snug but gently. Then, we attach the straps around his body so as not to interfere with his good wing. When the wind pushes against the artificial wing, it will stretch out just so. When he lands, it will close up, thanks to a little spring-loading device. It'll be awkward as hell, sure, but it will give him a chance to fly."

"It's wild," I said, smiling. I loved the idea. It was the sort of thing I would have wanted to do myself, only I wouldn't have had the know-how to do it.

"It's a gamble," Mr. Ryerson reminded me. "We might not be doing Jack any favours."

I thought about what it must feel like to be a bird up in the sky flying every day of your life. And then what it must feel like to be shot down out of the sky and not have any understanding of what happened to you. I thought about how unhappy Jack was in the cage. What if it was me? I asked myself.

I looked at Marina. "I say we give it a try."

"Good," her father said. "You hold him still. I'll fit the wing. I've checked the healing. Birds heal very quickly. I don't think this will hurt him." So, as Jack clamped down again on my glove, Mr. Ryerson, with great concentration and a lot of gasping, harnessed Jack into his new wing. It was folded in two at first and it looked totally absurd.

Mr. Ryerson sat back down in his wheelchair and caught his breath when he was through. "Cautious at first. Let's do this one step at a time," he said.

I set Jack down on the grass near the shore-line ever so gently.

At first Jack just stood there. He looked around at us. I swear he looked each one of us directly in the eyes. Then he stretched out his good wing, tentatively. He started to flap it and fell over sideways from the weight of the con-traption on his other side. But he got right back up.

I looked at Dad and he was shaking his head sideways. *No*, he was trying to tell me, *it isn't going to work*. The creep. Wasn't that just like him? Ready to give up, ready to admit defeat before Jack had a real chance. I clenched my fists just then but said nothing.

Jack was getting himself back under control. He started to flap away with his good wing again. This time he must have been remember-ing what it was like in the old days because the artificial wing began to jiggle about. Then as the wind under it began to work, it unfolded and stretched out to its full length, perfectly, as long as his real wing.

Mr. Ryerson was bent forward. "Come on . . . come on . . . you can do it," he was saying. I was holding my breath. Jack was flapping and flapping, and both wings were moving up and down, beating against the ground. I could feel the power of the bird as the wind spit out from underneath him. Then he just stopped.

And I thought that maybe he had given up. That it had been a really dumb idea, just like my old man thought. But instead, Jack started again, flapping and flapping and lifting his feet until he was just barely off the ground. He let out one of his famous shrieks and pounded away at the ground with both his wings until he was spinning around in a circle but going nowhere.

I didn't know just then if I was watching something magnificent or something pathetic. The loser in me said it was a bad joke, a nice try but a bad joke. The dreamer in me told the bird to forget about gravity and get his ass off and flying.

"Please, please," I heard Mrs. Ryerson say as the bird kept spinning around in a kind of frenzy.

"You can do it, Jack," my mom said now.

"Yeah, you can do it," Marina repeated.

I knew enough about flying to realize that if Jack was going to take off under such difficult circumstances, he'd have to be facing straight into the wind, not spinning around in a circle. Time to take another chance. Jack was watching me, watching all of us as he beat his wings against the ground. It could be a mistake to scare him at a time like this, but birds respond instinctively. I'd have to take the chance that his instincts were still good.

I walked quickly a couple steps towards him and clapped my hands loudly. He stopped his spinning frenzy and began to stumble, to run away from me towards the harbour, into the wind. As he ran, his wings began to flap again, this time with even more strength than before.

His feet came up, his wings still smacked the ground but he was moving fast. And as the ground dropped away near the shoreline, Jack's wings, one grey and one polyester blue, began to work the air. He skimmed the water but he lifted slowly but surely, wobbling a bit, faltering, then readjusting. But the bird was flying.

"I don't believe it," my father said, but he grabbed onto my mom and gave her a big hug, then jumped up and down and let out a hoot like a little kid.

I watched as Jack circled around in front of us, faltering again, trying to adjust to the wind, but seeming to relearn with every move. Test. Adjust. Compensate.

I could see from Mr. Ryerson's face that I was not just looking at a man with cancer stuck in a wheelchair. I was looking at a man who had wings.

We watched Jack fly around and around. I was afraid now that Jack might just take off and fly away for good. We all knew that his artificial wing was by no means permanent. Out in the wild, it wouldn't last. If he came back, if he could adjust to domestic life, the wing would be something that we could strap on to let him fly now and again. But I decided that if he didn't come back, maybe that was the way it would have to be. Jack's one last flight might be better than a life in a cage on the ground.

As we shielded our eyes against the sun and stared hard into the sky to keep up with the flight, my father retreated to the house and came out with a bag of frozen cod heads and gutted whole mackerel. *Jack's gourmet meal.*

My father was a believer again. He walked to the shore and held up one of the mackerel.

Minutes passed and I thought we had already lost Jack. Dad stood there like a crazy man holding a dead fish up to an empty sky. Then suddenly a big, gaudy, insane-looking creature swooped down over us from behind the house, snatched the fish out of my father's hand and landed on the water in front of us.

The wing had folded as designed but caused him to sit a little lopsided in the harbour. Jack took no time in wolfing down the entire fish, bones and all, as was his habit. When he was finished, he ducked under the water a couple of times and then paddled ashore.

His new wing was dragging a bit as he waddled up over the rocks past my old man and directly up to Mr. Ryerson. He came within a metre and then just stood there looking at him. Mrs. Ryerson had a handkerchief up to her face and was trying not to make any noise as she blubbered.

Mr. Ryerson was looking at Jack. "It worked," he said to the bird. "For once, it worked."

Jack didn't seem to be paying any attention. He stood perfectly still and lifted himself up on one foot, a seagull's at-rest position.

Chapter Twelve

It should have been a good omen. Jack's success felt like a turning point in my life. But the next day the real estate sign went up in front of our house.

The door to my father's office was closed. "Don't bother him," my mother said. "He's working on his résumé."

"I don't think we should move," I told her again.

Mom didn't say anything. She picked up the bucket of kitchen scraps and headed outside to the compost pile. I followed her.

My mother had a vegetable garden that was picture perfect. Neat rows. No weeds. It was a place of order, and I think it was one area of her life she had control over. She dumped her garbage into the composter and mixed it with dirt.

"You and Marina are a good pair, I can see that. But you're not going to win. If you keep at it, you're just going to get into more trouble. Steve and I don't want to see that."

"But I don't want to be like him," I said, pointing at my old man bent over at his desk by the window. "I don't want to go through life feeling whipped." I was still feeling pretty hostile towards my father.

My mom was stirring the compost in front of her. She stopped. I knew I had said the wrong thing and I guess I was ready for her to give me a lecture. Instead, she turned and slapped me hard on the face. "You don't talk like that about your father," she snapped at me and then walked away.

My face was stinging and I felt a mix of guilt and rage. So this is what it finally came down to. My parents, who always tried to be my buddies, were turning against me. They didn't like me trying to fight for what was right because they had lost before. They wanted me to be a wimped-out quitter like them.

I didn't want to go to work. The wind was light and out of the south. I got my wetsuit, rigged my board, and headed north on my windsurfer to Marina's house. I sailed east, then northwest back towards my side of the shore, trying to disregard the grotesque, smoke-spewing finger of the smokestack.

The sting of my mother's slap stayed in my head the whole way. My life at home was falling apart. I was thinking I could live without them. Let them move. I'd figure out some way to stay on here. Maybe I could live without them. Maybe I'd be better off.

Up ahead I saw a bunch of trucks parked on the government wharf. The place had been pretty dead ever since the fishing gave out. In the old days quite a few families used to make a living from going out to sea and catching cod and hake and flounder. Then, slowly but surely, there just weren't as many fish as there used to be. The wharf had been put in with government bucks in the 'seventies to try and bring things back to life. But it never worked. You couldn't bring back the fish by building a new wharf. So it had been pretty deserted for a long while. I came in close and a couple of guys waved to me, but I didn't wave back.

I knew that something was wrong here. I hadn't heard anything from the locals at the gas station about the wharf opening up again or about fishing being on the upswing. It was something else and I knew it wasn't good news. I didn't have to be a genius to put two and two together — to realize that the big concrete wharf went out into the deep water of the harbour. It was only a mile or so from the landfill. You could bring a barge down any number of rivers to the ocean, then down the coast and into Rocky Harbour straight to here. That way you didn't have to transport toxic waste on highways or on railway tracks that go through people's backyards. Out of sight, out of mind.

It was all part of some grand plan to turn Rocky Harbour into the waste-burning capital of the east coast.

Marina must have seen me coming because she was there on the shore to greet me. She gave me a big hug and for a few seconds I felt like someone had waved a magic wand and taken all my worries away. But for me and this crazy girl, it seemed that passion always had to play second fiddle to business.

I had almost forgotten why I had come here or what I had just seen at the wharf.

"I called the lab," she told me, "and said I needed the dead birds back as evidence. The guy I talked to before just put me through to his supervisor. That turkey told me they had disposed of the mergansers, that it was standard procedure."

"We should have thought of that before, I guess."

"But he also told me that they had made some kind of mistake with the lab report. A mix-up or something. He said that the report was wrong, just a goof-up. He offered to pay me the money back."

"My mom was right. It's not going to work." I looked over at Jack in his make-shift pen, thinking about how great it was to see him fly yesterday. And I thought of myself yesterday, out on the waves with the wind in my face, having the time of my life. "It's crazy," I said. "We've got too much against us. We're not going to get anywhere."

Marina seemed shocked. "What? Are you ready to give up?"

And I suddenly felt totally embarrassed. My head did a perfect 180-degree spin. I tried to fake a truly confident smile and shook my head. "We're in this together, right?"

"Yeah . . . I think so."

I was looking at her and wanted to say a whole bunch of stuff. I wanted to say that she was the best thing that ever happened to me, but I just couldn't bring myself to say it. Instead, I said something safe. "You really like a good battle, don't you?"

She shrugged. "Well, I was always fighting my battles alone until you came along."

"Really?"

"Back in Culverton, after my dad got sick, I tried to organize a demonstration against Dial Chemical. I knew it was their fault he was sick. And it just wasn't him or the other workers. They'd been dumping in the river for years. But too many kids in school had parents who worked there. I couldn't get anything off the ground. I couldn't even get some of the guys who kept trying to put moves on me to get into it. Nobody cared."

"I wish I'd been there with you."

"Thanks, but I don't think one more person would have made any difference. I went to the factory with a sign. I walked around by the main gate. I watched as all the men who used to work with my father drove by me and either ignored me or cursed at me. I don't think they knew who I was. But they didn't care. It didn't do any good at all. But I think I learned something."

"What?"

"Well, it was like that guy Gibson. There are a lot of people out there that don't want to hear the truth — especially if it involves their jobs. They think anybody who complains or raises a fuss does it just because they want attention, just because they're troublemakers. They can't understand that some people really care."

"I know that now," I said. And I thought it was pretty strange that once again, here I was with this girl I was head over heels in love with, and all we ever did was have these heavy conversations about all the problems with the world. What I really wanted to do was suggest that we go off somewhere and just make out, but that wasn't the way it was going to be.

"We have to go over Gibson. We have to go the next rung up the ladder."

"The Regional Authority? My father says it's like talking to a concrete wall."

"Well, the wall might have to listen. This authority thing is made up of mayors and county councillors. And they're elected. They at least have to listen. Ed Keller's the guy who's elected from here. He was an old friend of my father's when they were growing up. My father says Ed will listen. He already phoned him and Ed agreed to see Dad today. He just lives down the road and he's coming over for lunch. Ed knows my Dad's pretty sick. He couldn't say no. You want to join us?"

"Sure," I said. I checked my watch and was reminded of the fact that I should have been at work over an hour ago. "But first I have to use your phone and lie like hell to my boss at the gas station."

Chapter Thirteen

Lunch was not exactly a fun scene. Mr. Ryerson looked much worse than usual. He was the first to own up to it. "Every once in a while the chemotherapy really starts to take its toll," he said.

"Bill, shouldn't you be in the hospital or something?" Ed Keller asked rather bluntly. You could tell he was pretty upset at seeing an old friend looking like he was on his last legs.

"I should be but I'd rather be here. I'm loaded with all these different drugs. One to fight the cancer, one to try and restore my immune system. Another to keep me from throwing up, another to keep my heart stabilized. They couldn't do any more for me if I was in the hospital. I'd just lie around and feel sorry for myself."

Ed smoothed back his thinning hair and looked at the rest of us. He wanted to change the subject real bad. "So what are you kids up to this summer?" he asked Marina.

That was her cue. I could tell she was nervous but Marina wasn't going to back off from her plan. "We're trying to stop you from bringing in chemical waste to burn in your incinerator," she said matter-of-factly, looking him straight in the eye. "If possible, we'd like to close down the landfill and the incinerator altogether."

I had to control myself to keep from laughing as Ed choked on his food. Mrs. Ryerson looked a little embarrassed. But I saw a twinkle in the eye of Mr. Ryerson.

"You have a feisty daughter there, old buddy," he said.

I didn't want Keller to have a chance to change the subject too easily. He was a politician and a smooth talker. "There's a couple of big problems with that whole waste disposal site," I told him.

I waited for him to take the hook. "For example?"

"Well, for one thing . . . it leaks. Major deadly stuff like heavy metals are leaking into the ground water."

"I doubt that," Ed said politely. "We've got good men who designed that site. We hired the best environmental consultants money can buy to design the disposal field . . . "

"Excuse me, sir, but I think you're mistaken. You didn't hire my father and he was the best — is the best — and that's because money *can't* buy him." I was trying to throw Keller's own words back at him.

He looked at me and I knew that *he* knew just then precisely whose son he was looking at. "I assure you," he said, now sounding more than ever like a politician giving a speech, "that there are no problems with the landfill or the incinerator. It's all monitored on a regular basis."

"Tell that to the dead mergansers," Marina said and handed him a copy of the lab report.

Keller set his sandwich down, put on his glasses and studied the report. Mr. Ryerson didn't seem to mind that we were less than polite to his lunch guest. In fact, he seemed to be enjoying the spectacle.

"Where'd you get this?" he asked.

"We paid for it," I said. "We found the dead birds outside of the landfill. There's a leak in the clay liner where the ash is dumped. That ash is full of all kinds of deadly stuff, and it's probably finding its way into the harbour. I don't think your consultants had figured on that."

"Ed," Mr. Ryerson said. "I'd consider it a personal favour if you'd go over there today with these two and check it out." He began to slide his chair back, away from the table. He hadn't eaten anything the whole time we sat there. I knew from what Marina had told me that it was hard for him to eat normal food. The chemotherapy had its side effects.

And I guess Ed just couldn't bring himself to say no to an old friend who looked in such rough shape. "Sure," he said. "Why not? I haven't been there for a long while. Let's do it."

When Ed stopped at the Shell station for gas, I had to duck down so that no one would see me. Ed thought I was acting pretty weird but then he thought we were both pretty strange kids. "I never met a pair like you two before," he said.

"No, sir, I bet you never did," Marina replied.

Ed had phoned ahead and Gibson was there waiting for us outside the concrete building. "What are you doing with these two juvenile delinquents?" Gibson asked right out.

"Easy, Ron. These are two very intelligent young people. Marina here is the daughter of an old hockey chum of mine."

"I see," Gibson said. "Well, I had to call the police to haul these kids out of here the day before yesterday. They came around like they were on some kind of campaign or something and started accusing me of all sorts of things."

"Hmm," Ed said, not really wanting to get in the middle of a tangle.

"Under normal circumstances, we're quite polite, sir," I said to Gibson.

I looked around towards the landfill and I saw the bulldozers at work near the ash pit. I could see that they had carved out a large hole and were transferring the ash to dump trucks. The dump trucks were then trundling off to another part of the huge landfill.

"You believed us," I said to Gibson, pointing to the dozers at work. "You know we were telling the truth. The crud that comes out of that ash is leaking out of here and into the stream."

I felt a kind of rush go through me. For a minute I thought we were gaining ground.

All of us were looking towards the dozer at work now.

"Oh, that," Gibson said. "We're just doing a routine transfer of the old ash towards the centre of the landfill. Happens twice a year. We let it pack down, condense and then we bury it deeper and cover it up."

I was sure this wasn't the way things worked. They knew they had a leak and they wanted to fix it before it could be proven.

Ed was scratching his chin and trying to size up the situation. He took out the lab report and handed it over to Gibson. Gibson seemed un-flustered.

"I've seen this before. It looks convincing, doesn't it?"

"What do you mean?" Ed asked.

"I mean that I checked it out with the people at Quality Labs. They say they never did any tests on any birds. The best they can figure is somebody faked one of their lab reports. I'd say there's some pretty fancy con artists around," he said, looking at Marina and then at me. "You know, sometimes people just want to cause trouble for the sake of causing trouble."

I guess Marina had heard that line once too often, because even before I could respond, she let go and kicked Gibson hard in the shin. And I mean hard. Gibson fell over onto the ground and grabbed onto his leg. A couple of other workers nearby had stopped in their tracks and started laughing.

Ed looked really flustered. He held out a hand to help Gibson up. "I'm sorry about this, Ron. I didn't know this would happen."

"This man's a liar," I told Ed. "I also know why Quality Labs decided to change their mind about the report. Whoever tested the birds didn't know where they came from. But when his boss found out, it was a different story because this is their project. They did the study giving the okay for this landfill. And they're in on the new deal to burn the chemical stuff. Gibson and his men are fixing up the leak so that it will be harder for us to prove that this place is unsafe. But what about the next leak? And what about the next batch of dead birds or poisoned drinking water?"

Ed saw that I was getting red in the face and really losing my cool. But he didn't say anything to me. "I think you should apologize to Mr. Gibson," Ed said to Marina.

"Sorry, Mr. Gibson," Marina said and kicked Gibson again in his other leg.

Chapter Fourteen

Ed Keller said he would look into the situation at the dump, but I knew at that point that he didn't want any more to do with us. The big battles had been lost here a long time ago. The cards were stacked against us. I knew that we could still find evidence of the leaks if we wanted to take some more water samples. But I also knew that it wouldn't matter. No matter what we found out, there wouldn't be enough people around here willing to care, willing to stick their necks out and fight this thing.

I refused to talk about it with my parents. My dad had finished his résumé and told me he had a talk with a company out west. "People out there still care about the environment. It's not like here. Here it's too late." I wasn't going to give him the sad satisfaction of hearing about my day.

"I think it might turn out to be the same everywhere," I told him. "I don't think it's going to be any different. Besides, I'm staying. I'm not moving." I was thinking about Marina. Nothing like her had ever happened in my life. Nothing "out west" could uproot me from Rocky Harbour.

That got my old man really jangled and I felt a little guilty. But my life was one big confusing maze these days. I couldn't help it if I didn't have much sympathy for my old man.

I went to work the next morning and discovered that my boss, Bud Gilfoy, had seen me in the car with Ed Keller the day before.

"I'm sorry, Mr. Gilfoy," I told him. "Something came up. It was very important."

Gilfoy looked at me like I had just thrown up on his desk or something. I needed this job if I had plans to hang around after my parents were gone. It was time to grovel. "I'll work today for free. I'll wash every window of every car that pulls in here. I'll change tires. I'll do the work of two pump jockeys. Just watch. And I don't want you to pay me a cent. That's my form of apology."

Suddenly Gilfoy smiled. "I like your attitude, son," he said. "You're willing to admit you made a mistake. That's good. Now I hope you don't mind getting a little messy, 'cause I also want you to change the oil in my car and those four trucks out back. Then I want you to spray undercoating on my mother-in-law's Plymouth. After that I want to see them toilets scrubbed clean as a whistle. And all the while, if you hear a car drive in, you better be out there pumping gas like your life depended on it. Can you handle that?"

"Yes sir," I said. "Thank you, sir."

Gilfoy smiled a devilish grin at me and repeated again. "Yep, I like your attitude."

At the end of my morning shift, I was covered in grease and oil and I felt like crap, but I knew that I had made amends for skipping a day's work and lying about it. I was in the washroom trying to get the crud off with waterless soap when Bud stuck his head through the door and said, "You done good, Chris. My conscience tells me I'm going to have to pay you for today. Just tell me this. What the heck were you doing riding around with the county councillor?"

"I wanted him to see the landfill," I said. "It was polluting the ground water and killed some ducks." I wanted to keep my explanation simple.

Gilfoy shook his head. "That's not good. I like to shoot ducks. You make sure they don't go killing off those ducks or I won't have any Christmas dinner." But he was smiling like it was a big joke. I decided not to tell him what I thought about hunters.

I rode my bike on down to Marina's house. No car was in the driveway. Nobody was home. Jack looked up at me from his cage and shrieked a mighty loud hello. I knew what he wanted. He wanted another crack at the artificial wing and a trip up in the sky. When I went to the back door I saw a note taped to the glass. It was written in haste by Marina and barely legible:

Chris, My dad took a bad turn. We had to take him to Memorial Hospital. Marina.

Memorial was thirty miles away. I knew she needed me. And I had to get there. Now. I ran out to the highway and stuck out my thumb . Three cars passed but none of them stopped. I started jogging down the road. I knew I couldn't run all the way there. But I just felt that I couldn't stand there and wait. I wanted to be with Marina.

Two more cars passed me by even though I stuck out my arms and waved like crazy. They probably thought I was just that: crazy. I was getting desperate when I saw the Purolator truck coming over a rise in the road. I made a quick prayer that the guy had good brakes and decent reflexes. I jumped out in front of the oncoming van and waved for him to stop.

He slammed on the brakes and burned off some good tire tread coming to a stop.

"You lose your mind, kid?" he screamed at me.

"Please," I said. "I've got to get to Memorial Hospital. My girlfriend's there with her father. It's really important I have be there."

The guy looked me over. "It was you and the girl with the dead birds, right?"

"Yeah," I said. "Can you give me a ride?"

"I'm not supposed to have any passengers. In fact, I caught hell for taking those dead birds to the lab. We're not supposed to transport poultry."

"Come on, man, please? I need to get there."

He leaned over and unlocked the passenger door. "Get in. If I get in trouble, I'll be looking for you."

"Thanks."

I found Marina on the third floor. When her mother saw me coming, she got up and came to me. "Thanks for coming, Chris. Sit with Marina for a while. I'm going to talk to the doctor."

Marina had been crying. I put my arm around her, not quite sure if it was the right thing to do. "Are you all right?"

"No, I'm not all right," she said. "His cancer is worse. Much worse."

"Just take it easy," I said. "I'm sure there's something they can do."

She shook her head. "I know you're just saying that. You don't know what we've been through already. My father came back here to Rocky Harbour because he was dying. You can't possibly understand."

I had nothing to say. She was right. I didn't know. All I had were clichés. I wanted to help, but there was absolutely nothing for me to do except be here with her. "I wish I could help."

"Just hold me," she said. "Just hold me."

I was still holding her when Mrs. Ryerson came back. "Go in and see him," she said, looking at us. I let go of Marina and she got up to follow her mother.

"You too," she said. "Unless you don't want to. He'd like to see you, Chris."

I followed Mrs. Ryerson into a room and saw her husband in a bed lying flat on his back. He had tubes going in through his arm and one going up his nose. A monitoring machine of some sort was beeping. I knew for sure that I was looking at a dying man.

Marina put her head down on her father's chest and his hand came up to stroke her hair. I had never known this man when he was healthy, and I hadn't been around for his long and painful decline, but I knew that I cared about him. Ever since I'd seen his miracle with Jack, I knew this guy was amazing.

He wanted to say something, and he was looking at me. He whispered first to Marina.

"He wants to talk to you, Chris," she said. "He wants to speak to you alone."

Mrs. Ryerson seemed a little baffled but she led her daughter outside.

I pulled up a chair and sat real close to Mr. Ryerson. He was breathing hard. Every breath was a struggle for him.

"I'm glad you came," he told me in a quavering voice.

"How do you feel?" I asked. I wasn't just trying to make small talk. I wanted to know how much it hurt.

"The drugs deaden the pain. But my mind is sharp. I don't know how long that will last. That's why I wanted you and me to talk."

"I'll do anything . . . "

He nodded his head. "Good, you already answered my first question. Do you know why I came back to live at Rocky Harbour?"

I knew what Marina had told me but I couldn't bring myself to say it. "No," I said. "I mean, I'm not sure."

"It's okay. I came back to die. That part you know. And it's true. But there's more. There's you."

"I don't know what you mean."

"Marina says you're different from the others. You care about things. Like the way you saved Jack. You try to help."

"I don't think I have any choice."

"That's what I mean. Marina is the same way. She always was. I want you to hang around and help. She's going to need you."

"I'll be there," I said. And I knew just then that all of my threats to let my parents move off west without me would have to be made good. I couldn't move.

Mr. Ryerson took my hand and tried to give it a squeeze but he was weak. "Dying is the easy part," he said. "It's life that's hard."

I felt dizzy for a second as a wave of something powerful swept over me. Mr. Ryerson looked much weaker. I could sense him losing ground and knew I couldn't be the one here with him if he was to go now.

I opened the door and held it for Marina and her mother to come in, then sat myself down on the hospital hallway floor just outside of the door and waited.

When I heard Mrs.Ryerson let out a painful cry, I knew that the time had come. A doctor rushed into the room, but I just sat there feeling the cold concrete under my butt. I wasn't ready to move.

Chapter Fifteen

Even though I had known Marina's father for only a short time, I felt like I had lost a good friend. It's funny to admit this, but something about his death made me feel sorry for myself. I mean, it interfered with Marina and me becoming closer and getting to have fun. I wondered if we'd ever be able to have fun again. Ever.

I know that sounds stupid under the circumstances, but I felt cheated out of something. I wanted to have this boyfriend/girlfriend thing. I wanted to forget about the battles and about the destruction and now all the sadness. But it just wouldn't go away.

Don't get me wrong. I was there for Marina. I was ready and willing to help out with everything. Sometimes she wanted me around.

Sometimes she wanted to be by herself. I just went along with her moods.

On the day of the funeral, I nearly panicked. I almost couldn't handle it. My mother had ironed a white shirt for me and set out a tie and my old suit jacket. I hadn't worn any of that gear for a long while. The suit had always been too big for me, too bulky. Now it barely fit. The arms were too short and I could hardly get it buttoned. "No one will notice," my mom lied.

Putting on the tie did it. I was looking at myself in the mirror and I didn't look like me. Something had happened this last year; something weird was going on with me this summer. Suddenly I didn't care about Marina and her old man dying. I cared about me. And it wasn't fair.

I didn't want to fight the incinerator any more. I didn't want to have to deal with adults who didn't care how they screwed up. I didn't want to have to work at a Joe-job at the gas station. And I didn't want to have to go to some stupid funeral where adults would stand around being formal and polite and saying stuff that didn't mean anything at all. But above all, I thought, as I stood there looking at the goofball in a too-tight straitjacket of a suit, I didn't want to grow up.

"Time to go," my father said. He and Mom were driving me to the funeral.

Mr. Ryerson was the first dead person I'd ever seen up close. He was lying in a coffin, looking pale and somehow fake. The funeral parlour had lots of flowers and religious music coming out of big speakers in the walls. There were surprisingly few people there. I shook hands with some folks that I didn't know. Everybody kept saying how sorry they were.

"Marina, are you okay?" I asked her as soon as I could get away from my parents.

"No, I'm not okay. I don't think I ever will be." She was mad. She was very angry. "I don't want to be around all these people. Most of them I don't even know."

"Let's get out of here, then. Let's go outside."

"No. I have to stay here with my mom. I have stay with her."

I tried to put my arm around her shoulder but she pushed me away. "You can't take it all on yourself." I was trying to say that I wanted to help but she wouldn't let me.

She was about to cry again, and I didn't know what she wanted me to do. She sucked in a sob and took a deep breath. Then, looking at the wall, not at me, she said, "I want you to just leave me alone today, okay? I know you're trying to be helpful. But I don't like you feeling sorry for me right now. I need to be with my mother and I don't want you around — not now, not for a few days. I just want some distance, and I don't want you around."

"Why?" I asked, completely bewildered.

"It confuses me," she said. "I know you're trying to be a good guy, but I don't want it right now. I don't want to depend on anyone. And I don't want you around."

Then she got up and walked over to her mom. She smiled a fake smile at some people coming in through the door and acted cool as ice, unmoved.

I went back to my parents and we all just sat there doing nothing, saying nothing. There was a short service and a minister told some details about Mr. Ryerson's life — how he had grown up along the shores of Rocky Harbour and how he had "come home". He said that Mr. Ryerson had been a good worker, a good husband, and a good father. But it was all rather vague and it could have been a description of anyone. I kept waiting for him to say something real, but it didn't happen.

I wanted him to explain about the cancer that had killed this "good husband and good father". I wanted him to make the connection with Dial Chemical, but nothing was said. He missed saying everything that was important about the man. I wished I had the courage to stand up then and name Dial Chemical as the cause of the death, because this was all a big wishy-washy performance to make everybody feel better. It was all bullshit.

At the burial, I couldn't even get Marina to look at me. She was holding onto her mom and I could see that she was right. Marina was the stronger one; she was the one keeping her cool, her face like stone as her father was lowered in the casket into the ground.

When the last prayer was said, she led her mother to a waiting car and they were gone. When I looked back at my parents I was shocked to see that my father was crying. His head was bent over and his shoulders were shaking. I had never seen him cry before, and

I knew that he had only met Mr. Ryerson once. There was more going on here than I understood.

My mother drove us home and we all sat silently in the car. Then I went for a walk along the shoreline and skipped stones out into the water. There was a good wind up out of the southeast. I thought of going sailing just to make myself feel better. But it didn't seem right. Nothing seemed right. So I sat down on a rock and said her name out loud. Over and over. *Marina. Marina. Marina.*

Chapter Sixteen

Almost against my will, I turned into a good employee that summer: a good, quick fill-er-up pump jockey able to wipe a window, check the oil, and polish a pair of headlights before the automatic shut-off click had spit a dribble of gasoline up into the air.

I rode my bike at top speed to work first thing in the morning, working my legs until they ached and my lungs felt hot spikes of pain from pushing myself. I worked until noon, and then ate a couple of ham or liverwurst sandwiches with a pair of greasy fists while I sat around the station office listening to Bud Gilfoy tell fishing stories or dirty jokes. Then I raced home as fast as my legs could get me there and I went windsurfing.

Weather didn't matter. If there was only a trace of air, I drifted lazily around the harbour.

If there was a hurricane, I was out there, rip-snorting with the waves — pushing myself, pushing my board, making myself stretch the limits of my ability.

Some days, if the waves were breaking out on the sand bar, I took to sea and learned everything there was to learn about riding a sailboard on waves. I could dance across the face of a long, green wall. I could tuck hard into the freight train collapsing ridge of water, or I could vault up into the sky, straight over any piece of water the Atlantic could throw at me.

Once I got hammered in the side of my head with my board when I wiped out and came up seeing stars. Once my sail got cracked hard by a collapsing wave and I broke my mast. It was a long paddle home but the tide was with me, and that night I learned the art of fibreglass repair.

But the whole while, those two weeks of work and play were totally empty of anything that resembled real life. If you think I took any satisfaction from my work or had any fun on the water, you're wrong. I was just going through the motions. Marina and her mother had gone back to their old home town of

Culverton. The day after the funeral, I woke to find Jack outside my back door in my makeshift cage. Marina had returned him and left me a note:

My mom and I need to get away from here for a while. We might be moving back to Culverton. We're going to stay with my aunt up there while my mom looks around for work. Who knows what happens from here? Take good care of Jack.

On top of the cage was the artificial wing, but it was broken in three pieces. I think I understood what it meant. Marina had tried to get Jack to fly again and he'd crashed. Jack looked like he was okay. After all, he was a tough old bird. But I could picture in my mind how Marina must have felt. And now Jack, once again with a single wing and no chance of flying, was back with me.

All my efforts to track down Marina and her mom failed. The post office lady wouldn't tell me a forwarding address. The funeral director knew nothing. I sent Marina letters to her old address in hopes that they would find their way to her. But time slipped by and I received no answer.

And life went on. I got a raise; I could have turned into a windsurfing pro, and I could have won a national trophy in cross-country bike racing. But it was life in a dead zone. When a family came to look at our house and stand in awe at the view of the sunset from our back porch, I didn't even care. I didn't even bother to sabotage the deal with my prepared speech: "And guess what, folks? You have your very own landfill and incinerator just two miles up the harbour from here.What more could you ask for?" Nope. I didn't say a word. In the end it turned out that they didn't have enough money for a down payment. They were just "looking around". But the evening left my whole family feeling like we had been invaded. I think my father felt it the worst.

"They kept talking about *our* house like it was just some sort of *thing*," he said in a huff after they left.

Ed Keller showed up one night. "I'm sorry to hear about Bill Ryerson," he said. "I'll miss him. He was a good stickhandler in his day."

"Why didn't you come to the funeral?" I asked, remembering how few people had been there. I think it had made Marina and her mom feel more than ever like outsiders.

"I'm not good around death," Ed admitted. "I don't have the stomach for it."

"That's too bad," I said sarcastically. Ed had been nice to Marina and me, but he hadn't got us anywhere. He was just a politician and a gutless one at that.

I could see Ed was trying to ignore my words. "I came to tell you that I followed up on your complaint about the landfill. I'm not saying they did anything wrong. But I can tell you that they are going to clean up their act. They have to, now that they have the new contract with Dial."

I was wishing that he wouldn't remind me of that. Importing waste from away to burn at Rocky Harbour meant more smoke in the air, more lethal ash that wouldn't be looked after properly.

"The first barge arrives in two days. I know you don't see it from our point of view, but it's a big step forward," he said, trying to sound convincing.

"How do you figure that?" I challenged him.

"Well, we get to help rid the environment of chemicals that, up to now, have just been sitting around posing a health threat to people."

I wanted to say a lot just then. I wanted to tell him about Mr. Ryerson and his years at Dial Chemical and how Dial had refused to own up to any of the dangers he had been exposed to. I wanted to tell him that I didn't trust Gibson or anybody working at the landfill, that I didn't trust the Regional Authority and that I thought all his talk was a crock.

"How can you be hauling in the stuff when the second incinerator isn't even built yet?"

"Maybe it is a trifle early but work is already under way. And the government wharf is now in shape to handle the unloading. Everyone agreed that the waste would be safer on our site than at its current location right in the city there in Culverton. It seemed like a good idea to start shipping the stuff now. It would show real commitment from everyone involved. If you could only see the big picture, I think you'd agree that we are doing what's best for people and the environment."

I really wanted to flip out on this guy. All he had were words. And with those words, he'd try to make people think that they were all heroes for importing toxic waste to Rocky Harbour.

"Look," I said. "The incinerator that's already there isn't even safe for burning trash. Maybe there is a way to burn the stuff safely but not there, not with that equipment. Why should I believe the next burner you put in is going to be safe?"

Ed was cool. "We've hired experts — consultants. They assured us it would be safe. Do you really think I'd let this happen if I thought it was otherwise? Besides, it means more jobs and more revenue coming into the county so we won't have to raise property taxes."

"Those guys always tell you what you want to hear."

I guess Keller decided not to argue with me on that one. Instead, he said, "You know, you could get in big trouble for forging that lab report."

"I didn't forge it! If I had the money for a lawyer, I could probably prove it but what would it matter anyway?"

"You're lucky Gibson or even Quality Labs didn't want to press charges."

"Let them try."

In his own way, I guess, Ed thought he was trying to do the right thing. "I admire your cockiness," he said. "I was like that once."

"Yeah? Then what happened?"

"I guess I just grew up, that's all. It'll happen to you too. Just don't let your emotions make you do something dumb."

Just what I needed, a lecture from Ed Keller. "What did you come over here for, anyway?"

"I just wanted you to know that I took your concerns seriously. I checked into everything — there's no leakage of anything from the dump site. Everything is okay with the incinerator, and the new system will be nothing less than state-of-the-art. I asked hard questions of Gibson and the consultants involved. I didn't just do it for you but for Bill too, and his daughter. And I wanted you to know that everything is above board. No animals are going to die. Nobody is going to get sick. In fact, no one will ever even notice anything different around here."

Ed got in his car and drove off. I realized what he was trying to tell me about growing up. The trick was to stop worrying, stop noticing. Just stick your head in the sand and pretend that everything was going to be okay.

I went over and fed Jack some fish scraps left over from dinner. After he had gulped them down, I reached in and picked him up. I let him clamp his beak hard onto my finger and it hurt like hell. But I didn't pull away. In fact, I liked the pain. Like my angry confrontation with Ed Keller, it reminded me that I was still alive after all.

Chapter Seventeen

Two days later, I woke up saying her name to myself again. Why wasn't she here with me? This was her battle too. Heck, she was the one who got me into this. I got on the phone right away and called my boss.

"I can't come in today. Can you get someone to cover the pumps?"

"You sick?"

"No." Bud had treated me fairly. I wasn't going to lie to him.

"That's good. I don't like to hear about my employees getting sick. Usually means they're not eating enough of the right kind of foods."

"It's not that."

"What is it?"

"The first barge of chemical garbage comes in the harbour today from down the coast. I want to be there."

"You still afraid there'll be more dead ducks?"

"Yeah."

"Man, that could screw up this year's hunting season real bad." Bud was teasing me again. "You tell those turkeys that if they kill off my ducks I'll come down and shoot their ass."

"I'll tell 'em," I said. "Thanks." And I hung up, thinking that even if I didn't have any strong allies I at least had a few people around who didn't think I was crazy.

My parents were off to do the food shopping and meet with the real estate people. Somebody from away had put a bid in on our house without even coming to look at it. The bid was low but my parents wanted to talk it over with the agent. I gave them one bit of advice before they left: "Don't sell. This is our home."

Dad just let out a long sigh and looked down at his shoes. My mom shook her head and I know she wanted to give me one of her little motherly bits of advice but she didn't say anything.

When they left, I went out to feed Jack. I had fixed the artificial wing that Mr. Ryerson had made, delicately repairing the tube frame with fibreglass and sewing (yes, sewing) the dacron where it was ripped. I think it was as good as new. But I wanted to wait for Marina to be there with me when I let Jack fly again. It was illogical. As each day passed it looked less likely that Marina would ever return, that I'd ever see her again. I guess I was being a little cruel to old Jack by keeping him caged. But I had other things on my mind.

Once the Regional Authority had made its decision about disposing of "imported" chemical waste, there had been very little fanfare about it all. Ed Keller had tipped me off about the first barge coming in. Nobody was in a better position than me to keep an eye out for it. I decided to pack some food and go up on the hill behind my house to the little rock ledge that had a clear view of the entrance to the harbour. Down by the shoreline I had my sailboard ready. I was pretty proud of the job I had done on the sail. In big, bold black letters, taking up every inch of the sail was the message:

ROCKY HARBOUR — NO PLACE FOR CHEMICAL WASTE

Long ago, I had given up on trying to enlist allies. With Marina gone, I was on my own. But if I was willing to take the risk that I was about to take, I realized I needed an audience. I needed someone to know that I was making a stand, that I hadn't just rolled over. So I phoned the news desk of *The Daily News* and spoke to a young reporter named Nick Wheatley. I explained to him who I was and what I was about to do.

"I don't know," he said. "That whole incinerator thing is a dead issue. We gave it a couple of stories a month or so back. You can't keep beating a dead horse. The public has lost interest."

"I know all about the public losing interest," I said. "Maybe there's no story here at all. But think of it this way: this is the first barge of this sort to ever come up this harbour. Heck, Ed Keller calls this an 'environmental breakthrough'. That's got to be worth something. And you could get a great shot of the barge coming in the harbour mouth just as some maniac kid on a windsurfer — namely me — takes his life in his hands by blockading the harbour on a sailboard."

on the rock. I sat down and took my shirt off. The sun was warm on my chest and I felt a momentary charge of nostalgia for the old days of being a kid, daydreaming away the hours here in the summer sun. The forest used to be full of wildlife — squirrels and spruce grouse and rabbits, maybe a deer or two. This morning there had only been the snake. And now I thought about how sitting in the sun like this was, in itself, something dangerous. I had the ozone layer to worry about. Potential skin cancer. And what else was already in the air that I was breathing, what fumes from the incinerator? After the new stack got built, it could be ten times worse. I put my shirt back on. I wondered if I was going to have to invest in a gas mask. Why the hell was it that nothing was as simple as it used to be? Why was it that we were willing to take so many chances?

Noon passed and I had tucked myself into the shade of an overhanging maple tree. My eyes ached from squinting through the binoculars. I was feeling lazy and tired. The adrenalin had leaked away, and I basically felt like taking a nap. All my anger and enthusiasm was gone, drained down into the rocks I was sitting on.

An old familiar voice was inside my head telling me my plan was stupid. What could I hope to prove? I was a loser, right? I felt like I always lost everything I cared about. I had even lost Marina and it wasn't even my fault. Now I'd lose this place, this harbour, the place I called home.

That's when I saw the black smudge out to sea, a dark plume of diesel smoke. I put the binoculars up to my weary eyes and peered through, trying to get past my blurry double-vision. It wasn't a container ship headed to Europe and it wasn't a Coast Guard ship. It was boxy and squat like an army tank but distorted by that shimmering mirage effect of the sea, magnifying it several times its real size.

I let the binoculars fall to my chest. The loser was still in control of my brain cells telling me I might as well forget it. Lay down and take a nap with the snakes.

Then I heard this loud shriek that nearly burst my eardrums. It could have been one of Jack's war cries but I knew he was too far away, down safely in his cage. I thought for a split second it might well have been one of the bald eagles, who flew above this ridge in search of food. But it wasn't that either. I discovered that this call of the wild had come out of me. And suddenly I was wide awake. And I heard an echo to my cry from down below. Jack had heard me and he was letting me know that he understood.

I had shouted down the loser, and he was retired inside my brain somewhere. My heart was pumping and the floodgates of adrenalin were wide open. I had met the first enemy and it had been me. Now I was ready to do battle with this black thing on the horizon. We had a rendezvous and I sure wasn't going to miss it.

I sprinted down the hillside, kicking loose some stones that scattered and rattled as I ran. Running through a forest, downhill, on a rocky, root-strewn trail was a skill I was good at. I could have done this with my eyes closed.

"Nick," I said on the phone. "I've spotted the barge. Can you be there?"

"You bet!" he said, sounding a little more enthusiastic. "Hey, my editor isn't too keen on this. In fact I don't think he wants me to get involved. He's got a brother working at the plant but listen . . . " and he suddenly began to whisper. I could picture him cupping his hand over the phone. "I called the wire service. They say that if I can get a good shot of you in direct confrontation, they might want to run it."

"What's that mean?" I asked.

"If it goes out over the wire, then you could get your picture in every paper in the country."

"Try to get my left side," I said. "That's my good one."

"Just be careful, kid," he said.

"I know what I'm doing," I lied and hung up.

Chapter Eighteen

The wind filled the sail and pulled me onto my feet as soon as I hit the water. It was my harbour, my home. I was headed out to protect this place, to do battle with some sort of sea monster.

Did I have a plan? Yeah, I had a plan. I would put myself between the barge and its destination. I would make my point loud and clear to whomever was running that ship that it was not wanted. The words were on my wing. I believed in the unbelievable as I skidded across the surface of the water, lighter than a bird, more invulnerable than a rhinoceros. I believed that I could somehow get out there, show them that they were *wrong*. And that they'd turn around and take their deadly payload back to where it came from.

In other words, I had lost all my common sense.

But I wasn't thinking reasonably just then. I wanted to prove my point. The wind was brisk and kind. I tacked north, then south and east, and finally out through the channel, past the dead-end road on the far side of the harbour mouth.

It wasn't just the wind that was pulling me along; it was the fire that bloomed inside my chest of a never-again loser who was about to prove that he could win and that he could go it alone if he had to.

My nerves were like dancing wires of raw electricity. I cruised out into the ocean and off towards the sand bar to the south. The waves. The sparkling, cracking, hollow, little waves. There I shot up into the air, I danced along the face of them, I swooped and swayed like the gulls around me as the barge neared the harbour mouth. I wanted them to see me. Nobody could miss the yellow and blue sail. I wanted whoever was on that barge to see me here first, to see me snapping up into the sky in rebellion of gravity. To see me racing along the sea at the speed of light. I wanted them to see I was no ordinary, mortal human being. I was someone capable of feats of the impossible. And the forces of sun and sea were my allies.

The barge slowed as it neared the harbour mouth. I saw two men on deck. Inside must have been a third piloting the big, ugly crate. They saw me. They saw me loop a high arc up into the sky as I shot over the top of a metre-high wave and come down for a perfect splash-down. They saw me and they were saying to themselves that they had never seen anything like it in their lives. I'm sure of it. They saw some crazy kid performing aerial manoeuvers like he was living on a planet with zero gravity.

I popped over top of my final wave and grabbed the wind with my sail, rocketing to-wards the barge now. I was tucked low, har-nessed in, barely hanging onto the sail in a downwind crusher-race to beat the diesel-breathing engine to the harbour mouth.

As I came up close from behind the barge, I watched as the two guys in overalls read the message on my sail. I tried to speak, I tried to shout, but at first nothing came out. The diesel engine was a dull roar now as I came up behind the barge and jumped the wake on both sides like I was water-skiing behind the boat.

The two men were smiling at me. I didn't like that. They thought I was out here fooling around. They were missing the point. I surveyed the load of barrels. Barrels of poison destined to be pumped up into the sky. I pulled in alongside the boat as close as I dared. I pointed to the message on my sail.

One guy nodded. Yeah, he'd read the message. He stuck his middle finger up in the air at me. I saw the contortion of anger on the other guy's face as well. I could see the man in the steering house now and he gave me a hard look from behind his sunglasses. I was holding an easy position parallel with him, and I was hoping I'd have enough speed to keep up with the barge which was now moving along at a better clip than I had expected.

I faded away from the barge as we entered into the harbour, trying to make up my mind what to do next. That's when I saw the car pull to a stop up ahead at the end of the west road. A guy was jumping out with a camera. Nick had made it. I waved and he waved back.

Just then the barge captain gunned the engine. The stack blew out a dark, ugly cloud of smoke, and the engine growled as its prop chewed away at the water. I was losing ground and had to circle back around the barge, jumping the wake on each side until I was on the other side of the boat in a better position to use the wind.

"Go home!" I shouted to the men on board now. I had found my voice. "You're not wanted here! We won't let you wreck this place!" I don't know why I said "we." There was only me out here.

Who knows if they heard me. I knew that I hadn't done anything more than slightly annoy these men. Later they'd have a good laugh. And that would be it. Nick was up ahead, though. He was already snapping off pictures with his camera that had a big telephoto lens. In another minute the barge would have passed him by. Time for my move.

I dug in my foot and made a turn. The wind was driving me now. I matched the speed of the barge and then I went faster. I was vectoring in towards the barge again. I'm sure that from on deck it looked like I was ready to smash right into the side of it. But I pulled in even harder on the sail, gained more momentum. I had a terrible split-second of doubt, and whatever trace was left of my caution made me unhook my harness. If I was going to go down, I didn't want to be tangled up with my board and sail.

The captain of the boat saw me coming at him, saw me picking up speed and heading straight for an intersect path. But I would be slightly ahead of this black, charging monster. I would put myself in its path. I knew that if the wind let up even a whisper, I'd lose my speed.

We were directly in front of Nick now who was out on the rock seawall. I jammed the tail again and cut directly into the path of the barge. "Go home!" I shouted at them again at the top of my lungs.

Everything happened so fast. Maybe I thought that they'd actually listen. That they would kill the engine and let me talk to them, tell them why they should go home and not leave their deadly load here at our harbour. But they probably figured I was just a crazy kid who was bluffing.

And suddenly I was where I had aimed myself to be. I was directly in front of the barge as it continued to barrel ahead. And I hadn't counted on the power of the outgoing current of the tide that was working against me. I had a split second of awareness that I wasn't going to make it. I heard the engine throttle down, but I saw dark, cold steel plating right at eye level and knew that I wasn't going to make it. I prayed for a sudden gust of wind from the right direction to save me. But my prayer wasn't answered.

As the weight of this ugly monster bore down on me, I ditched the sail and I dove. I didn't even have time to get an honest gulp of air. I dove away and I dove deep. But I had the terrible feeling that it was all over, that I wasn't going to make it this time, that losers never do have a fighting chance after all.

Chapter Nineteen

I went as deep as I could and, as I tried to swim away, it felt like I was being pulled back. Underwater, fear crept up into my brain, and I wanted to scream. All of my courage for this impossible protest was gone. The truth is I was sure I was about to die. I was pretty close to drowning when I came back up gasping for oxygen. And I was so scared I couldn't see straight. I had swallowed plenty of water and I was gagging, too. But I forced my arms to move as I swam for my life to get to shore. Nick had waded out into the water to help me, but as soon as he saw that I wasn't going to drown he started talking about winning some sort of award with his picture.

My rig was pretty busted up. It had been mauled by the barge. As I got my senses back, I fished out what was left of my windsurfer.

The board had a big gouge taken out of the fibreglass and the sail was ripped apart. The boom was bent and mangled. I don't know why I was worrying about my gear. I should have just been happy to be alive. Maybe I was still in shock and not thinking too clearly. I tied it all onto the top of Nick's car and he shuttled me home.

"I thought you were a goner," he kept saying.

"Me too," I said, shaking and coughing. Finally I threw up. Fortunately for Nick, I rolled down the window in time and saved his seat covers.

The picture was never even run in *The Daily News,* but as Nick had predicted it found its way into papers all over the country. It showed me on my windsurfer just inches in front of the blunt nose of the charging boat of chemical waste. The message on the sail was perfectly clear. The caption read: "Lone Environmental Radical Tries to Stop Chemical Death Barge."

There wasn't even really a news story to go with it. Just a couple of lines beneath the caption that said:

*An overzealous youth tried to stop a barge
from entering Rocky Harbour yesterday
where it was delivering its first shipment of
toxic waste for disposal at a proposed incinerator. Although the barge collided with the
windsurfer, the boy, identified as Chris
Knox, was unhurt.*

"Unhurt" was possibly stretching it. Physi-
cally I guess I was okay, but I had nightmares
about that crash for a long time to come.

I never told my folks what had happened,
until the phone calls started coming in. A couple
of them were from people in other parts of the
country who had tracked me down.

One guy, who sounded a bit flipped, just
said, "Hey man . . . I wanted to call and just tell
you, right on. I think you had real guts to do
what you did. It's gonna be up to kids like you
to save the planet. Keep it up." He never told
me his name or where he was calling from, but
I could tell from his accent that he was probably
from out west.

I had a couple of calls from wackos who
called me all kinds of names. "Who hired you

to pull off that stunt?" one of them asked. Another said, "You just want to cause trouble and get your name in the paper, that's all. Jerk!" And he slammed down the phone.

"Don't answer the next one," my mother said. But when it rang, my old man picked it up.

"No, he's not here," Dad said. "I'll pass on the message if you like . . . um hunh. No, that won't be necessary. Yes. Okay, I will." And he hung up.

"What was that one about?" my mother wanted to know.

Dad looked at me and made a face. "It was a woman this time. She said she thinks you are very brave. She said she had phoned Nick Wheatley and found out you had your board chopped up. She offered to buy you a new windsurfer."

"What did you say to her?" I demanded.

"I said that it wouldn't be necessary."

"I don't believe it," I said and stomped off. The rift was growing again between my parents and me. We were light years apart.

My father stomped after me to my room, walked in and slammed the door behind him.

"You could have been killed, Chris. This has all gone too far. I can't allow it. You've got to give it up. You have to learn when to quit."

"Advice from an expert, right?"

"Yeah, maybe," he said. "But I got burned before, remember, burned bad. My whole career got put on hold . . . who am I kidding? . . . it got flushed down the toilet when I went up against the system. You . . . you're just a kid. Imagine what can happen to you."

"I don't know. What can happen to me?"

"You could get put in jail. You could get yourself killed. Who knows?"

"Ask me if I care," I told him smugly. Trying to block the barge was something I felt good about — all of it, including the nearly-getting-killed part. I had been scared to death and I hadn't backed down. And now I even had people from all over thinking I was a hero.

The phone rang again. My father rolled his eyes and started for the door to answer it. Then he stopped dead in his tracks and turned around. "No. You. I'm sure it's for you. Just don't say anything stupid."

"Hello?"

"Chris," she said. It was the voice I had been longing to hear. In the back of my head had been this insane hope that my picture in the paper just might . . . "Chris, I saw the photograph. It really scared me."

"What do you mean, scared you?"

"Are you all right?"

"Yeah. I'm fine," I said. "Well, as fine as I can be without you. I miss you."

"I miss you too and I'm sorry I haven't gotten in touch. I just couldn't deal with things. And it had nothing to do with you. You were the best thing that ever happened to me. I just had to be away from there. And I had to put all my energy into helping my mom. I really had no choice."

"I understand," I said, even though I didn't. Part of me wanted to yell and scream and kick and tell her how much *I* had been hurting, how it wasn't my fault her dad had died so why was I being punished? But I didn't say it. I wasn't as stupid as everybody thought I was.

"Chris, I need you here. I can't come back to Rocky Harbour, not just yet. But, please . . . is there some way you can come here? I don't want to explain it all but it's really important."

"What is it? You have to tell me something. I mean, sure, I'd do anything just to see you. I'll come, but what is it? What is it you're not telling me?"

"You thought you were all alone out there, didn't you? You thought you were the only one left in the fight, right?"

"Yes. That's exactly how it felt."

"You were wrong. You're not alone. And it's not all over."

Chapter Twenty

The bus ride to Culverton seemed to take forever. I sat there realizing that this would be the end of my job at the Shell station. I had called Bud Gilfoy to tell him my situation but I knew that I was stretching his patience. I couldn't even tell him when I'd be back. Now I wondered if I ever would be back. I knew I was going to be with Marina again and that's all I cared about. Whatever pain she had caused me, I forgave her. Because now she needed me.

I sat beside a bad-smelling guy on the bus who snored the whole way there. Most of the trip, I just stared out the window. The spruce forests and hills near Rocky Harbour were behind us. We were on a big highway driving past rows of houses all looking the same. Then there were a few highrise apartment buildings and low, ugly concrete bunkers that were surrounded by tractor trailers. I wondered why anyone would want to live around here. There were almost no trees, no lakes. Nothing but trucks, cars, wires everywhere and man-made ugliness. It was beginning to sink in what a sheltered life I had led.

It took most of the day to get there. When I got off the bus, though, Marina was standing there waiting. She ran to me before I even had a chance to figure out what do. She threw her arms around me and squeezed hard.

Her mother was standing off in the crowd. She looked about ten years older than when I'd seen her last. I smiled at her and continued to hug Marina.

"How's Jack?" Marina asked.

"Not getting much attention, I'm afraid. My mom is looking after him while I'm gone but she says she doesn't trust him. I can't say I blame her."

"The only person Jack ever really trusted was my dad."

"That's true. Your father was like a saint."

It was really awkward hanging around Marina's aunt's house. Her aunt and her mother were trying to be so polite and nice to me but I could tell they felt uncomfortable having me there. I wasn't part of the family. After dinner, Marina and I went for a long walk. She held tightly onto my hand as we walked through a run-down neighbourhood until we came to a high, rusty, chain-link fence surrounding some sort of factory.

We walked along the perimeter of the fence until we came to the entrance. The gate was locked. The sign read: *Dial Chemical, a Division of Consolidated Holdings. 120 Days Without an Accident.*

"They're very proud of their safety record," Marina said. "They're good at covering up the real truth."

"So this is the place?" I saw a bizarre assortment of pipes running into several sooty brick buildings. There was a strong, unfamiliar stench in the air.

"That's what killed my father," she said. "We just couldn't prove it."

"It's still pretty painful, isn't it?" I asked her.

"Yes. The pain doesn't want to go away. But it doesn't hurt as much when I think about doing something about it."

"What do you mean?" I suddenly had a vision that she wanted me help her sabotage this huge, ugly factory. What would I do if she asked me to blow the place sky-high? I guess I was giving her a pretty funny look.

She could read my mind. "Not that. Maybe I fantasize about doing that, but I'm not as brave and wild as you."

I guess I blushed just then, feeling a little proud that she saw me as an environmental terrorist. "What is it then?"

"I'll explain when we get home. I just wanted you to see this place."

"It's a real tourist attraction."

"It's a dinosaur," she told me, "but it's not extinct yet."

"Your father wasn't the only one, was he?"

"No," she said. "You can go down to the library and they have the statistics on file. It doesn't take a genius to figure out why this town has such a high cancer rate. Other diseases too. It's pretty obvious."

"But there are jobs at stake, right? Dial Chemical is pretty powerful."

She shook her head. "Read the sign. Consolidated Holdings is pretty powerful."

"I don't understand."

Just then a security truck pulled up to the gate from the inside. The truck had a searchlight on top, and the guard must have seen us in the dark snooping about. He aimed the light right at us but Marina had grabbed onto me and was kissing me hard on the mouth.

She didn't pay any attention to him when he caught us in the spotlight and said, "Get out of here, you kids. Go find some place else to make out!"

When we got back to the house it was only ten o'clock, but everybody was asleep. "Follow me," she said and we crept through the house as quietly as we could. She led me into the bedroom she slept in and gently closed the door behind her.

The room was pitch black and I could sense her standing very close to me. The only sound was the two of us breathing. It was a situation I had dreamed of.

"Chris," she whispered in the dark, "this is a little complicated to explain, but I need you to promise you'll keep a secret."

I swallowed hard. "Promise," I said.

She switched on a lamp and sat down at a little desk. From the drawer she pulled out a large manila envelope.

I now noticed that the picture of me from the newspapers was cut out and taped to the wall over her desk. Marina handed me some papers that she'd slipped out of the envelope. "Look at these," she said.

At first I had no idea what I was looking at. Some kind of legal documents with small type. The only thing that made sense were the words, *Consolidated Holdings,* in the top centre.

"When my father was working for Dial, he was really proud of his work. It seemed like a crummy job to me but he took satisfaction in doing what he was told to do and, strange as it may sound, he liked the company."

"So?"

"So he bought some stock. First in Dial and then, when it got bought out by Consolidated, he became a shareholder in Consolidated Holdings. It's a multinational company that owns all sorts of things, but Dial is one of its big money-makers."

"I'm in over my head. Your father owned part of the company that killed him?"

"It was only a tiny part, but he made a profit as an investor like every other shareholder in Consolidated."

"I never spent any time thinking about business stuff," I admitted. "I don't have any idea how this works. You mean you just put up some money, buy some stock and then start making money?"

"If the company is doing well."

"But how could it have been doing well if it was slowly killing its employees and polluting the air and water at the same time? I mean, they've been stockpiling toxic waste here for nearly a decade, if I understand it right. Until the Rocky Harbour incinerator came along, they didn't even have a plan as to how to get rid of it."

"Well, they used to just dump it in the river until some of the loopholes in the law got taken care of. And to answer your question about making money, I know this much. Shareholders want profit and most of them don't care how the profit is made. It's the name of the game."

"It sucks," I said. I was still looking at the papers in front of me and finally, now that I knew what I was looking at, I noticed something else incredibly weird. "This stock is in your name!" I said.

"I own a small part of that godforsaken corporation," she told me.

"How? Why?" I asked. I had a sudden fear that Marina had gone way off the deep end.

"After my father got sick, he knew he wouldn't live for very long. So he put some things in my mother's name, some in mine."

"Doesn't it feel all wrong?" I asked.

"No," she said. "That was part of why I called you. It feels very right."

Chapter Twenty-one

I don't get it," I told her. Maybe she had completely wigged out.

"Take that look off your face," she said. "Don't worry. I'm not crazy. At least I'm not as crazy as someone willing to get run down by a barge for kicks."

"I was proving a point," I said, pretending to be a little hurt.

"I know. Now it's my turn. Flip to the last page. Check out the listings of other holdings."

I turned to the end. There it was. There must have been thirty or forty companies in all.

"They're called subsidiaries," Marina said, sounding like a real expert. "One big company owns a lot of smaller companies."

"But it's still like the same people running the thing."

"You got it. Keep going through the list."

Then I came to one I recognized. "Quality Consultants," I said out loud.

"Who wrote up the study of the incinerator in the first place and later advised the Regional Authority that it would be all right to build another burner for chemical waste."

"And who also run Quality Labs?" I added.

"You're beginning to get the picture."

"It's got to be illegal, right?"

"I don't know. I'm not sure. I do know that it's not *right*, but I don't think we can prove anything is illegal."

"That's what my father used to say. He was up against this sort of thing all the time. Until he burned out. He still wants us to move away from Rocky Harbour."

"You're not really going to leave, are you?"

"Why? What difference does it make now? You're not there, and even if you go to the papers with what you have, people around Rocky Harbour won't get upset. They don't care any more."

Marina pulled out a folder from the desk and opened it. She handed me the copy of the lab report and the copy of my father's incinerator evaluation that I had given her. Then she reached to the wall and pulled the newspaper photo of yours truly off and handed it to me.

"Maybe we don't even have to deal with the Regional Authority or any of the bozos of Rocky Harbour." She pointed to a calendar on her wall where the tenth of the month had been circled in red. "That's tomorrow," I said. "What's gonna happen tomorrow?"

"It's why I wanted you here. I don't think I can do this alone. But I can if you're there with me."

"Where?" I wanted to know.

"There's a stockholders' meeting of Consolidated Holdings here in the city. Tomorrow. Downtown at one of the big hotels. I'm going to put this before the stockholders. I'm going to let them know what's going on."

There was fire again in Marina's eye. The same anger, intelligence, and energy I had seen the day we first met when she started blaming me for the landfill. "But you already said that all the stockholders care about is making profit. They want money. They don't care about the rest."

"It's a gamble," Marina said. "But we've got nothing to lose. I kind of doubt if any of the big guys would care but maybe there are a lot of little people like us who show up at these things. Maybe they will care."

"You're crazy," I said.

"You gonna help?"

"Your wish is my command," I told her and when her mother opened the door to see what we were up to, we were kissing again for the second time that night.

Mrs. Ryerson cleared her throat, giving me a nervous, suspicious once-over. "I think it's time you both get some sleep. I'll just remind Chris which room is his." And she led me down the hall to the little bedroom where I made a valiant attempt to get to sleep, my head spinning with the thrill of having returned to the world of the living. The world that included Marina. The world of fighters, not losers.

Marina had even borrowed a suit from a cousin for me to wear. At first I told her: no way. But she convinced me that we needed to try to fit in. It was bad enough that we would be the youngest people there. The suit was too tight and I felt like a real twerp. The tie was choking me. I couldn't believe that businessmen

dressed up like this every day. It was real
punishment.

On the up side was seeing Marina all
dressed to the teeth. She looked even better
than she did in her wetsuit.

"Wow!" I said. "You look beautiful."

"You've never seen a girl dressed up before?"

"Not one like you. You'll knock 'em dead!"

"That's precisely what I want to do."

"Marina," Mrs. Ryerson cut in, "are you sure
you don't want me to come with you? You two
might get yourselves in trouble."

"No. Thanks, Mom. I'll be okay as long as
Chris is there."

Mrs. Ryerson gave me a doubtful look. "I
always keep my cool," I told her. "If anything
goes wrong, I'll be there to keep things under
control. It's my specialty."

Mrs. Ryerson just shook her head and
walked out to the car.

"I definitely don't want my mom there. It
would be too hard on her confronting the
people from Dial."

"I can imagine," I said. "But what about you?
Are you sure you can handle this?"

"Yes."

Man, I'd never been in a building like this before in my life. The hotel was brand spanking new. Mrs. Ryerson dropped us off at the front door. Some turkey in maroon tails opened the car door and the door to the lobby of the hotel. I felt like I was suddenly up there with the rich and famous. It sure was a long way from Rocky Harbour.

But the whole time we were walking through the magnificent lobby, my brain was making these crazy leaps. Something was coming together in a way I had never expected. I pulled Marina over to sit down for a minute on a little sofa. There was a mirror on the wall behind us and I caught our reflection in it. We both looked older, more sophisticated. We looked like two people I had never known and everything behind us in the mirror world was like something I had never imagined: chandeliers, paintings on the walls — rich, rich, rich.

"What is it?" Marina wanted to know. "Why are you acting so weird?"

"I always act weird when I look in the mirror and see that it's not me there but somebody else. But that's beside the point. While we were walking through the lobby, I was just thinking. I was thinking about the link between all this and the incinerator at Rocky Harbour." But then I stopped. I wasn't quite sure what I was going to say.

Once again, it was like Marina was reading my mind. "I think I know what you're getting at. Everything here is so clean, so orderly, so sophisticated, and under control. There's nothing here that is like Dial Chemical. There's nothing dirty."

"Right. And when those people sit down in that room over there, they won't be thinking about any barge load of deadly chemicals that's going to burn in a second-rate incinerator that will pump poisons into the sky."

"I know. This is all unreal. That meeting in there will discuss profit and loss. It will have nothing to do with the reality of chemical waste. No one will be thinking about what happened to my father."

"And that's why we're here, yes?"

"We're the reality factor."

Chapter Twenty-two

Another lobby zombie in a maroon suit was standing by the door to a large assembly room that went by the name of *Salon Westover*. He had his eyes fixed on us as we approached. At first I thought he was just checking out Marina because she looked like such a knock-out.

But when we reached the door, he singled us out of the crowd.

"Where are you going?" he asked us.

"To the shareholders' meeting," Marina answered.

"I'm not sure it's open to kids," he said.

I wanted to plant some knuckles in his face, but Marina squeezed my hand and I knew she wanted me to be cool.

"I am a shareholder," she said. She started to root around in her bag for the certificates she had brought with her just in case something like this happened.

There was a crowd behind us and we were holding up traffic. The guy didn't feel like hearing any explanations. He didn't want us in there because we were just a couple of kids. "I've been directed to keep out anybody who doesn't belong here. Do you mind stepping aside?"

I had enough from this jerk. "Look, buddy," I said, trying to play it tough. "You have no right to stop us from going in." Other people were looking at me now and I realized again just how much I didn't fit in. My voice was all wrong. I had said the wrong thing. Rats.

Some old lady behind us in the crowd seemed to take the delay pretty personally. She shoved ahead and, in a voice full of indignation, said to me, "Young man, what are you doing here causing all this trouble? You should be ashamed of yourself." She must have been pushing eighty years old. She had on a long flowing pink dress and grey hair stacked up like a cloud on top of her head.

I couldn't see what her problem was and why she wanted to get involved. I was about to tell her just that.

"I'm sorry, Mrs. Jennings," the guy in the maroon uniform said. "Please go right in. I was just about to get rid of these people who don't belong here."

She glared at me and then began to walk on but Marina grabbed onto her sleeve. "Wait a minute," she said, holding her stock certificates with her other hand. "I have as much right to be here as you do!" There was fire in her voice as she looked the old lady right in the eye. I was almost afraid the woman was going to have a heart attack.

Oh boy, we're in big trouble now, I was thinking, and we hadn't even got inside the hall. I half expected the goon would now have us arrested. Instead, this Mrs. Jennings looked at Marina and said, "Who *are* you, anyway?"

"It doesn't matter," she said. "We have a right to be here just as much as you do."

And with that, the old lady's indignation faded and she suddenly smiled. She turned to the baffled man who had stopped us. "Why won't you let these young people in then?"

"I don't think they belong here," he said.

She turned to Marina and ever so calmly said, "I'd like to introduce myself. I'm Mrs. Benjamin Jennings and I've been coming to these meetings for much longer than I care to admit. You look like a fresh face in this tired crowd. May I ask what brings you to our little gathering?" (Already there must have been at least five hundred people at the "little gathering".)

"My father left me some shares in Consolidated when he died," Marina said. "And I always wanted to come to a shareholders' meeting."

The woman put two hands up in the air and smiled as if to say, "Where's the problem in that?"

"And this is your young man?" she asked pointing towards me.

"That's him," Marina said.

"Then let them pass, and don't be so pernicious," she said to the bozo who had tried to stop us.

As we walked in and found a pair of seats in the middle of the room, I wondered what the old lady would think of us once Marina had spoken.

Marina and I looked over the package of papers we had been given. It might as well have been in Chinese. Numbers, charts, graphs, long paragraphs talking about "competitiveness", "efficiency", "innovation", and of course, "profitability".

"Now what?" I asked Marina nervously.

She thumbed through the papers until she found the agenda and pointed at an item called *New Business*. The meeting began. *New Business* was way down the line. We needed to be patient.

Patience was not one of my skills. I fidgeted, I squirmed, and I began to wonder what the heck we were doing there. Why did Marina think that any of these people would listen to us? They were almost all old. The faces looked dry and dead. The whole stupid meeting was as lifeless as a dead codfish.

Marina seemed oblivious to it all. She sat and she waited. And then the moment came. "The floor is now open to new business," the bald guy up front said. Chairs were pushed back and men began to get out of their seats. But Marina had them all beat. We were already close to the microphone in the middle of the hall. She was on her feet and standing at the microphone before I could wish her good luck.

"Mr. Chairman," she said, "and ladies and gentlemen shareholders of Consolidated, you've never seen me before but, like you, I'm a shareholder." She paused just then and suddenly I realized how scared she actually was. I was almost afraid that she wasn't going to continue. Everybody was watching her. She took a deep breath. "My father worked for Consolidated, for Dial Chemical in particular, for over twenty years." The words came out slowly. Her voice was sounding shaky. I was nervous for her. My knees were jittery and suddenly I realized that she hadn't told me exactly what she hoped to achieve here. What could she possibly say that would make a difference to *these* people?

"Up to now, we've all heard what we wanted to hear. We've heard about profit, and we've heard about growth. Now, I'm here to tell you what real price has been paid for that profit and growth."

I watched people shift uneasily in their seats. I saw the "chairman" up front lean over and whisper something to the man beside him. Marina was oblivious to all this. "For years, Dial Chemical has been manufacturing its products and creating toxic byproducts in one form or another. Up until about ten years ago, I don't think anyone even cared about this. Now, times are different. People do care. But no one knows exactly what to do about it. So the most toxic waste has been put in barrels and stored on site here in Culverton in hopes that someone would come up with a good solution.

"Earlier this year, Dial thought it had found the solution for disposing of the waste. They found a town that had an incinerator in operation burning trash. And they found that the people in charge of running the incinerator and the dump there were ready to put in a second incinerator and import our chemical waste to burn for a fee. Dial has already begun to ship the barrels there by barge to the site at Rocky Harbour. I've brought along a resident of Rocky Harbour, someone who loves that place and has lived there all his life, and I yield the floor to him so that he can tell you about it."

It came as a shock to me. I blinked and found myself getting to my feet. Why had she brought me into this? I was no good at this sort of thing. Why was she doing this to me?

But, seeing as I had no choice, I shuffled up to the microphone and introduced myself. I felt the blood drain out of my face and for a second, I closed my eyes. I was about to freeze up when from behind my eyelids I saw a vision. It was Rocky Harbour on a beautiful summer morning. And I heard myself begin to describe it.

"When the sun comes up, it sends a long red trail out across the harbour. You can hear the sound of gulls and loons and smell the salt in the water if you stand by the shoreline. My house is right along the shore. Every morning it's different and every time it's wonderful. One morning I saw a whole bunch of young sea birds called mergansers learning to fly. They slapped their wings and legs across the water for more than a kilometre. If you keep looking, you'll see a kingfisher or maybe an osprey make a dive deep into the clear, clean, blue water and catch a small eel. Tall spruce trees grow along the rocky shoreline. If you look closely you'll see little red squirrels, maybe a racoon or two, porcupines, and rabbits. Rocky Harbour used to be a good place to fish." I looked around at the faces and I couldn't tell what they were thinking. They were just staring. "It's been changing, though. It used to be a good place for wildlife. And for people . . . "

Someone stood up just then. A big guy with a dead cigar in his mouth said, "Mr. Chairman, I object. We didn't come here for a lecture on nature. Let's get on with the meeting. I ask you to use your authority to shut this up so we can get on to more important business."

Marina was beside me now. She spoke directly into the microphone. "I would now like to complete my statement," she said.

The chairman was looking a little perplexed. "Perhaps you two young people have said enough and we should get on."

"But we're not finished," Marina said.

"I think you are," said the chairman and I saw his little wooden hammer in the air about to come down.

That's when I felt a hand on my arm pushing me away from the microphone, and I think I was feeling so frustrated right then that I was about to turn around and plant a fist in the face of whoever it was. But as I wheeled around I discovered it was Mrs. Benjamin Jennings. She took over the microphone and spoke abruptly. "Mr. Chairman, I can't let you just cut off these young people who have come here today. So far, this is the most interesting thing that has happened here since I started attending meetings over thirty years ago. I must insist you allow them to finish."

Again the chairman looked flustered as a murmur went up in the crowd. I detected a few voices saying, "She's right," and "Let them speak."

Obviously whoever this grand old lady was, her opinion carried some weight, because the chairman simply said, "Then proceed. . . . "

Mrs. Jennings bowed and stepped back. It was Marina's turn again. She stood at the mike holding up two documents in her hands. Her hands were shaking and her voice wobbled as she began. "When the first incinerator at Rocky Harbour was built by the Regional Authority, two reports were filed, one by Quality Consultants favouring the incinerator, one by another qualified environmental engineer saying the incinerator was not safe. Only the report that favoured the incinerator was accepted. I don't need to remind you that Quality Consultants are part of the holdings of Consolidated.

"Even then, the technology for the incinerator was old. It would indeed pollute the air, and the ash from the incinerator would be toxic. Now we jump ahead to the present. The technology of the chemical incinerator is also outdated and considered by unbiased researchers to be unsafe. The landfill is not equipped to dispose of the resulting ash safely. It has already been proven that water from the ash pit at the dump site contains heavy metals and is polluting the ground water and the harbour, killing birds and other wildlife." She held up the original lab report on the dead mergansers.

"And now *another* study by Quality Consultants has approved of this second incinerator to be used for burning the toxic materials of Dial Chemical, a company in desperate need to get rid of the waste it is still producing." Marina sounded totally in control now. Her voice was strong and confident. "I'm sure you can begin to see the deadly game that is being played here. And I say that, as shareholders of this corporation, we have no right to destroy a place as beautiful as Rocky Harbour just for our own profits."

She stopped there. I kept waiting for her to say something about her father but she didn't. People in the audience were talking to each other. Marina had made an impact but it looked like things were just going to move on.

"Seeing as there is no motion on the floor, we will move onto the next speaker," the chairman said. Suddenly we both realized that something had gone wrong. Marina didn't know the proper code words here. She hadn't "made a motion".

A man in a blue business suit was about to speak at the microphone, "Mr. Chairman," he began, only to be pushed aside by Mrs. Jennings.

"Excuse me," she said, "but I would like to put the motion on the floor. Our young shareholder has certainly made her case. And I don't think that we have to pretend that we didn't know about the problems with pollutants and toxic waste at Dial's factory right here in Culverton. We've been making many lawyers rich trying to defend our company against lawsuit upon lawsuit, from workers and citizens alike. In light of what has been said here today, I would like to put forth the motion that Dial ends its shipment

of chemical waste to Rocky Harbour or anywhere else. And we order the directors to under-
take a complete evaluation of the safety of the
Culverton processing plant — including its environmental impact."

Marina raised her hand and seconded the
motion. The old woman walked over to her and
gave her a hug. A couple of men stood up at their
seats and shouted, "Objection. Objection!" But
they were promptly booed by a goodly chunk of
the audience.

The room began to erupt into a frenzy of
shouting and arguing. By the time the chairman
had regained order, someone had proposed that
a secret ballot would have to be taken on the
issue. And while I had little faith in this roomful
of money mongers, I was sure that there would
be reverberations from this meeting for many
months to come for Dial Chemical.

As Marina and I sat back down I could see
that her hands were still shaking. And even
though there must have been hundreds of people
looking at us, I put my arm around her shoulder
and held her close but said nothing at all. I just
didn't think words were necessary right then.

Chapter Twenty-three

But there never really was a vote. It got bogged down in some legal technicality that a lawyer present from Consolidated brought forth. After the meeting, Mrs. Benjamin Jennings walked us outside, one arm around each of us. "It's not over yet," she said.

I rode back to Rocky Harbour in the car with Marina and her mother. No one talked much on the way back.

"We haven't made up our minds yet as to where we'll live," Mrs. Ryerson told me. "It will be a joint decision for Marina and me. I just don't know if Rocky Harbour is the right place. There are just so many . . . " She paused and groped for the right word. "So many *feelings*. I just don't know."

I was pretty surprised that Bud told me I could come back and pump gas in the mornings. I guess he had a soft spot for me and my effort to save the ducks. "You're a hard worker," he told me on the phone. "I'm willing to keep you on. Just stop taking so many gosh-darn vacations."

I read *The Daily News* each morning when I got to work and kept an eye out for articles written by Nick. Nothing much exciting. He covered a softball all-star game, the opening of a supermarket and a story about house break-ins. But then one day I saw something that made my heart skip a beat. I couldn't believe the headline: DIAL PULLS OUT OF DEAL WITH REGIONAL AUTHORITY. Front page stuff and Nick had the by-line:

A company spokesman for Dial Chemical has announced that his company has decided to pull out of the agreement to have its chemical waste burned at the proposed Rocky Harbour incinerator. Dial cites inaccuracies in the original study concerning the facility and an impending change in company policy towards waste disposal as discussed at a recent shareholders' meeting of the parent company, Consolidated Holdings.

A Dial spokesman suggests that there is "little or no" possibility of renegotiating the deal. A clause in the original agreement allows Dial to pull out without penalty. Councillor Ed Keller, with the Regional Authority, says that the construction of the second chemical waste incinerator "is put permanently on hold." He adds that, "locally, this will mean a loss of many jobs slated for the construction work and at least twenty permanent jobs at the facility."

Many people around here reading this article would think it was bad news. Lost money, lost jobs. But I understood what it meant. Dial didn't want the bad publicity with the public or with its shareholders. The Regional Authority was left holding the bag.

Bud was sitting at his desk engrossed in the sports pages when I grabbed his paper and forced his attention to the first page headline. He read it out loud.

"This mean they won't kill off all the birds?" he asked.

"Maybe," I said.

"Then I'll still be able to shoot some geese for Christmas dinner."

He knew how important the headline was to me. He was just trying to rattle my bones. I wasn't about to get into a debate about hunting right now.

"Watch out. One of these years, those geese are gonna start shooting back."

"Probably some crazed environmentalist will figure out how to teach 'em to do just that."

"I gotta go," I said. "Can you get someone to cover for me?"

Bud looked real annoyed, but then he always looked annoyed. "Only if you work two hours for the same pay as every hour you take off."

"I'll work four hours for every hour I take off."

Bud smiled. "Deal."

I got on my bike and burned rubber all the way to Marina's. I had the paper under my arm. When I got there she and her mother were packing.

"You can't," I said. "You can't leave. We won." I handed her the paper.

Marina started to cry as she came over and put her arms around me. "We did it," she said.

"Yeah, we did it. You and me."

But she kept crying, harder now, sobbing into my shoulder. I could feel her whole body shudder. "I just wish my dad could be here for this. I just wish he was still alive."

And then Mrs. Ryerson, who had been standing watching us, broke into tears and had to go outside.

"I think we still have to leave," Marina said. "It feels wrong here without him. We can't live in Culverton either. That would feel wrong too. We have to go somewhere different. We have to start over. It's what my mom wants."

"Is it what you want?" I asked, brushing the tears out of her face and kissing her lightly on the cheek.

"That doesn't matter right now. What I feel doesn't matter. I'm so glad for you . . . for us. We did something good. But I don't know if it really changes anything."

"It changes everything," I said. "But let's not talk about it now. I want you and your mom to come over this afternoon. We'll have a picnic at my house, out by the harbour. It's not often we have a chance to celebrate, so let's celebrate while the celebrating is good! You can't say no."

And I didn't give her a chance. I called home.

"Hi, Mom."

"Chris. We heard. It's amazing! Your father is going wild. It's the first time I've seen him this happy in years."

"I'm bringing Marina and her mom over for a picnic. Okay? We want to celebrate."

"You bet. I'll get working on it. It's just what we need — a celebration."

Chapter Twenty-four

It was a warm sunny summer day along the shores of Rocky Harbour. My mom had set all the food out on the picnic table and my father was cooking hamburgers on the barbecue already when we arrived. For once everybody seemed happy. I think I knew that we had not won a total victory. Environmental battles are never completely won. Something else would come up. And there was still the problem with the incinerator site and the dump as it already existed. It was still pumping God knows what into the air and might still be leaking heavy metals into the ground water.

But even my old man didn't want to talk about the downside of things. We all ate and made small talk. It was like we were one big happy family.

"The agreement runs out with the real estate company tomorrow," my dad said. "I'm going to take the house off the market and wait and see."

"Way to go, Dad," I said.

"Hey, we're still broke. Don't look so happy."

"What about you two?" my mom asked Mrs. Ryerson. "Any plans?"

I was wishing she hadn't asked.

"We've decided that we want to start fresh. Somewhere else. It's not that we don't like it here, it's just that . . ."

"It's just that we feel we might be better off somewhere new," Marina concluded for her mother who seemed at a loss for words again.

I wanted to shout and scream at her. I didn't want to lose this girl who had taught me so much, this girl that I was in love with. But I chewed my hamburger and kept my mouth shut.

Jack was watching us eat and he let out a squawk. He wanted some attention. He wanted some food, too. My father, who had become quite attached to Jack while I had been gone, poked a fork into one of the left-over hamburgers and took it to Jack. The great one-winged gull lunged at the food and swallowed it in two gulps. "We'll have to rename him Burger Bird," Dad said.

Right then I remembered something. It hit me like a lightning bolt.

I ran into the house and returned with a pair of heavy gloves and the wing — the incredible artificial wing devised by Marina's father. I had repaired it a while back but never had a chance to try it out. I prayed that Jack still remembered how to fly.

I handed Dad the gloves. "Hold him nice and still," I said.

Trying to hold Jack still and fit the wing was like wrestling with an out-of-control weed whacker. But eventually I got it adjusted right.

I took Jack from my father and yelled, "Stand back!" Jack was like a bomb about to go off. I couldn't believe the power in him. Deciding that he stood a better chance of success if he was already in the air, I tossed him up high over the edge of the harbour.

He flapped frantically, lopsided, out of control. He beat his good wing and at first the other wing looked like it wasn't going to pull itself open. But Jack could feel the freedom of the sky and he flapped harder. The wing opened. He caught the air just inches above the harbour's surface, slapped his wings down hard on the skin of the water and began to fly.

We watched as he rose higher and higher in the sky, gaining speed and grace as he flew. Jack circled back high over us and squawked and squawked. Then he flew west so high into the sky that we all lost him looking into the sun.

"What if he doesn't come back?" my mother asked me.

"He wanted to fly. I had to take that chance. Again." I was looking at Marina. I was thinking about her father and thinking about us. I would have to tell her. Later. Tell her that I loved her wherever she had to live, whatever she had to do.

A car pulled up the driveway and stopped by the house. My first reaction was fear that this was somebody coming to look at our place. It was still listed. What if they made an offer? Would Dad change his mind?

Then I recognized the guy walking towards us. It was Ed Keller.

"This should be very interesting," Dad said to my mom.

"Congratulations," Ed said, looking at Marina more than me. "You kids lost the Regional Authority a lot of money. Too bad your folks are going to have to get stuck with higher taxes." There wasn't any real anger in his voice, though. It just came out sort of matter-of-fact.

"We did what we had to do," Marina said.

"I know," answered Ed. "And, in truth, I respect you for it. Just don't tell anybody else on the Authority I said so. In fact, they already think that this is partly my fault. I took you two kids to see Gibson, remember. I don't think they trust me any more. I'm no longer one of the boys." It was an odd thing to say but it suddenly occurred to me that Ed was trying to prove to all of us that maybe he was really on our side.

But I could tell my father wasn't convinced. "You have my sympathy," he said sarcastically.

Looking at my old man, Ed said, "When we asked Dial what evidence they had that we weren't running such a perfect 'environmentally friendly' operation down here, they faxed us a copy of your report — all one hundred and fifty pages of it. Seems that maybe we should have taken your advice way back when."

"I'm still available for hire," Dad said.

"Well, I don't think you'll have much more competition from Quality Consulting. No promises, but come by Monday and we'll talk."

"You're on," my father said.

Ed was looking off into the air over the harbour. He saw some giant winged creature like he'd never seen before flying towards him. Staring into the sun, he couldn't quite figure it out, but it had a really weird way of flying. And it was heading straight towards us. I guess Ed thought it was on the attack. "What in the name of Sam Hill is that?" he asked and started to edge sideways to get behind a tree. Then he watched as Jack dropped down out of the sky and landed on the ground in front of us. The landing was a little clumsy but Jack righted himself and casually walked past all of us, giving Ed a careful once-over as he made his way to the picnic table. He craned his neck upward and saw one lone hamburger sitting there. But he didn't grab it. He looked over at my father.

"What the heck," my Dad said and handed Jack the burger.

"I've never seen anything like that," Ed said, pointing to the wing.

"It was my father's idea," Marina said.

Ed understood then. He must have remembered his childhood buddy, his old hockey mate. "Bill always did know how to make something good out of a bad situation." He started to walk away but then stopped in his tracks, turned around, and looked at Marina and me. "Listen, I shouldn't do this, but I wonder if you'd both like to take a ride with me?"

"I don't understand," Marina said.

"The Regional Authority gave me the pleasant task of making a social visit to the director of the landfill. Thought you two might care for a return visit. I feel like I owe it to you."

I had a feeling that it might be pretty foolish for Marina and me to go visiting that place right now but it was too late. "You bet," Marina had already answered. "Let's go."

The look on Gibson's face as we walked into his office could have barbecued another round of hamburgers. The man was not a pretty picture.

"Ron," Ed said. "I came to tell you that you're fired."

"What?" Gibson said.

"Sorry. We know about the leaks and we know about the cover-ups and I don't reckon it's all your fault. We've all been turning our heads the other way. But we made some mistakes and now we're going to try to fix things up as best we can. Starting with you. So you're through."

"You can't do that."

"I already did," Ed said. He pointed to us. "I thought you might be gentleman enough to apologize to these two."

Gibson just glared at us and walked out of the room.

"The man's got no manners," I said. Ed just laughed.

There were no more barges to challenge at the harbour mouth. The water finally got warm enough that I could go windsurfing without all the neoprene gear. September was coming around. Marina and her mom packed and then unpacked three times. Mrs. Ryerson was still having a hard time. Marina herself wasn't sure if they would stay on for a little while and then move or if they were going to stay for good.

"I love you either way," I said. And I knew I could handle it. We'd been through it all. Nothing could change the way we felt about each other.

I knew the summer would end. One way or the other, things would be different. School was just around the corner.

But there is this day — this one incredible, wonderful day that is frozen in my memory. This one scene is locked forever in my head and in my heart and will keep me sane and keep me warm through all the dull, dead days of classrooms ahead. And it goes like this.

The sun is out. A warm, clean wind is pumping along the coast from the southwest. Marina and I are on our windsurfers, headed out of the harbour mouth into the blue, blue ocean. The waves are breaking on the sand bar, folding over into beautiful, blue tubes of water as the white spray flies up into the air.

Above us Jack is alive on the wind, a master again at flying. He tags along with us like an old friend. He has the sky; we have the water. We all work the power of the wind.

I've taught Marina a thing or two about riding waves on a windsurfer. Now she's already hotter than I am.

We cruise out past the headland until we feel the full force of the wind on the open sea. We hop over the whitecaps, our boards like flat stones skipping across the sea. Finally we carve a turn and make for the waves. We ride close to each other, in perfect sync. Then, when we feel the sea heave upward as the swell rises beneath us, we pull in on the boom and make off like lightning, sliding down the face of a two-metre wave. She scoots out ahead, I slip back near the collapsing wall of water.

I can taste the salt as the water whips up into my face. It tastes like freedom and dreams. As the wave collapses all at once, we both kick high onto the wall of water and let the wind grab our sails like parachutes. We are both out of the water and into the sky. We are flying. It's all a matter of perfect control, perfect free fall. We've learned the secret to tapping the endless energy that exists all around us and within us. Maybe it's only here and now. Just this wind and these waves. But maybe it's bigger than that. Maybe this is just the beginning.